THE EX
WHO GLOWED
IN THE DARK

Sally Berneathy

The Ex Who Glowed in the Dark
Copyright ©2013 Sally Berneathy

ISBN-10: 1939551110
ISBN-13: 978-1-939551-11-5

Chapter One

Amanda Caulfield walked out of the Dallas County Courthouse into the warm July morning feeling as if she was floating down the sidewalk on gossamer wings rather than clomping along in a pair of scuffed motorcycle boots.

She'd entered that intimidating building half an hour ago as Amanda Randolph, estranged wife and widow of Charley Randolph. She emerged as Amanda Caulfield, the name she was born with.

Her father wrapped an arm about her shoulders. "You okay, Mandy?"

She looked up at him, smiled and returned his hug. When Emerson Caulfield sat in the courtroom, his stern, no-nonsense demeanor quelled the rowdiest defendant. On the bench he looked every inch a district court judge with his stubborn jaw, strong nose and steel-gray hair, but now his gaze was soft, his parental concern for her obvious.

"I'm fine, Dad. Really. Getting rid of Charley's name makes me feel like a new woman, like the last few years never happened."

"That's just great, Amanda," Charley said. "Not bad enough I got murdered, but now my wife gets rid of my name and says she feels like a new woman and I never existed. You sure know how to hurt a guy."

Amanda grimaced and glanced past her father to the slightly translucent figure floating a few inches above the ground and scowling. Other than the translucence, Charley looked much as he had in life—tall with streaked blond hair and bright blue eyes. He still wore the tan khakis and white Polo shirt he'd died in two months ago. Apparently people didn't sweat or get dirty in the afterlife.

Ridding herself of Charley's last name had been a simple matter requiring the completion of a few forms and a quick appearance in court. If only she could get rid of Charley's ghost that easily.

She shot him a glare then continued walking down the street with her father toward the parking lot where his car and her motorcycle waited. "Thanks for going to court with me, Dad. It was kind of cool that you were on a first name basis with my judge."

Her father laughed. "A name change hearing is a formality, a matter of signing the decree. I was only there for moral support."

"That counted for a lot."

They stopped at a red light.

"Coming by for dinner tonight?" It would have been a tempting invitation if Amanda hadn't already made plans. Her mother always hired good cooks, her definition of assuring that her husband and family were well fed. "Your sister and David will be there. Your mother wants to make plans for the baby shower you're going to give for Jenny."

That took the temptation out of the invitation.

"Golly gee, Dad, I'd just love to be there and talk about which engraver to use for the invitations because remember what a terrible job Ludlow's did on poor Amy Cresswell's wedding invitations—how embarrassing that they used ecru instead of ivory—but Hamilton's has only been in business ten years and can you really trust such a newcomer, and should we stick with cardboard for the cake flavor or be avant-garde and go for lemon cardboard?"

Her father tried to give her his courtroom-stern expression, but he smiled in spite of himself. "You know you might as well give in and get it over with. Your mother is relentless. Eventually you're going to have to deal with the baby shower details."

Amanda rolled her eyes. "I know, but I'll avoid it as long as possible. Anyway, this afternoon Sunny and I are going for a bike ride and then out to dinner to celebrate my name change."

Her father nodded, his expression tightening slightly. "I'm glad you're spending time with Sunny, getting to know her."

Amanda had only recently learned that her mother and her birth mother were not the same person, that Sunny Donovan and her father had a brief relationship thirty-three years ago that resulted in her. Once she recovered from the initial shock, Amanda accepted her changed parentage without trauma. She'd always adored her father, always felt close to him, but she and her mother had clashed from her first memory.

Sunny made no attempt to take her mother's place but had immediately become her best friend, a role no one had filled in Amanda's life since Billie

Jean Bennett moved to Florida in the second grade. Overall, the situation was a good one.

The traffic light turned green and she and her father crossed the street to the parking lot.

"Tell Mom I'll be over soon with a bottle of two dollar champagne to celebrate Jenny's future baby and my old name."

Her father laughed. They both knew her very proper mother would not approve of a celebration of such an unorthodox event as ditching her dead almost-ex-husband's last name, and she'd faint if a bottle of two dollar champagne came through the door of her perfect home in Highland Park. "Let me know before you do that so I can be out that evening."

"Love you, Dad." She gave him another hug and a kiss on the cheek.

"Love you too. Ride safe."

She strode to her Harley.

Charley settled himself on the back and looked smug. "You can't get rid of me just because you don't use my name anymore. You're still my wife. Our divorce wasn't final when I died."

Amanda groaned and spread her hands in a gesture of frustration. "Think about what you just said. You died. What part of *till death do us part* do you not understand?"

"I'm still here so I guess death didn't part us."

"It's not my fault you got kicked back. You're definitely dead. Your family and I buried you."

Charley flinched. "That suit was terrible."

"Get off my bike. You don't need to ride. You can fly. Everybody wants to fly. You can do it but you choose to annoy me by riding on the back of my Harley."

"C'mon, Amanda," he whined. "You know how I used to love to ride motorcycles. This has been a traumatic day for me. It really hurts that you got rid of my name. At least let me ride."

Like she had a choice. She strapped on her helmet, fired up the bike and roared away. No point in trying to throw him off or give him a rough ride. Until he completed the mission he'd been sent back to complete or got his karma balanced or whatever he needed to do to be allowed into the light, she was stuck with him. Letting him ride on the back of her bike was a minor irritation compared to the other things she had to tolerate from him.

൞

Twenty minutes later she pulled into the parking lot of her shop, Amanda's Motorcycles and More, in the northwest section of Dallas off Harry Hines Boulevard.

"You ride too fast," Charley complained as she got off the bike.

Amanda yanked off her helmet. "Really? Are you worried I'm going to have a wreck and you'll get hurt? Next time, walk."

With her helmet under one arm and the folder containing her official documents under the other, she turned and strode toward the wide doors of her shop. Charley had put a damper on her good mood, almost made her feel guilty about getting rid of his

5

name. But a few minutes with her assistant and friend, Dawson Page, would restore her happy feeling. Dawson had been with her through the last year of her tumultuous marriage and her futile attempts to obtain a divorce. He'd appreciate what this day meant to her. They might very well share a two dollar bottle of champagne.

"Dawson, I'm Amanda Caulfield again!" She walked across the large open area, stepping around motorcycle parts as well as bikes in various stages of repair and detailing. She'd expected to find her assistant working on a paint job, his specialty and favorite thing to do other than play on the computer. But he was nowhere in the main area.

She finally found him sitting at a battered wooden desk in one of the smaller rooms she'd designated as an office. Not surprisingly his attention was focused on a computer, though not the desktop she had for office work. He'd brought in his own laptop, something he often did because her computer was, to quote Dawson, *antiquated*.

She stepped inside the room. "There you are! Did you hear me?"

Dawson jumped, looked at her over his laptop, blinked a couple of times and pushed his glasses up on his nose. "That's great, Amanda." He sounded distracted, but he often sounded distracted. Dawson gave his complete attention to everything he did, and at the moment, his computer had his attention.

Even so, Amanda was a little disappointed he didn't show more enthusiasm about her triumph.

Charley darted past her to stand beside Dawson. "He probably thinks a married woman should keep her husband's name."

Amanda bit back a response since Dawson couldn't see or hear Charley and would think she was talking to herself. Instead she stepped over to the desk and swiped the file folder containing her name change documents through Charley's midsection.

"That hurt, Amanda," Charley protested. "Okay, maybe not physically but emotionally. You've got a mean streak."

Charley had the roles reversed. In life he had been a liar, cheater and blackmailer. He was the one with the mean streak, but again she bit her tongue and saved her rebuttal for later when they were alone.

She slapped the folder onto the desk. "Dawson, could you put this somewhere safe? It contains very important papers. I don't want to lose them."

As a certified nerd Dawson always had more computer pallor than Texas tan, but now his face was pasty pale. His short dark hair looked as if it hadn't been combed in a while, and even through the lenses of his glasses she could see that his eyes were bloodshot with dark circles underneath.

A stab of guilt shot through Amanda. She'd been completely wrapped up in her own world and had failed to notice that something was wrong with her friend. "Are you okay?"

"What? Yes. I'm fine." He picked up her folder and set it down again. His eyes darted to the computer screen then back to her.

7

Amanda frowned. "What's going on? What are you working on?"

"Nothing."

That was totally not like Dawson. A college student majoring in computer science, he usually took every opportunity to explain anything related to computers in excruciating, convoluted detail, his enthusiasm blinding him to the fact that Amanda's eyes were glazing over while he talked.

She moved around the desk to look at the screen.

Dawson closed the laptop, blinked and looked guilty.

Something was very wrong. He wasn't the type to hide things from her and she'd never before seen him look guilty. "Dawson, I don't care if you were playing solitaire or looking at nude women." She couldn't imagine him doing either but what other reason could there be for him to shut down the display so she couldn't see it?

"Amanda, you know I wouldn't do that." He sounded hurt and indignant that she'd accuse him of such things.

"It wasn't pictures of women or a computer game or anything normal," Charley said. "It didn't have any of those little things you can click on, just lots of numbers and letters."

Okay, so not porn or computer games. Amanda felt helpless. Obviously something was wrong and it somehow involved whatever he'd been doing on the computer.

How could she help him when she didn't know what the problem was? She fell back on Texas tradition. When in doubt, offer food and drink. Dawson already had an open Coke sitting on his desk so she couldn't offer that. "It's nearly eleven which is nearly noon so why don't you take a break and grab an early lunch?"

Dawson shook his head, the movement uneven, half nod, half shiver. "I'm not hungry. You go ahead."

Dawson never passed up a chance to eat. Apparently it took a lot of calories to operate a keyboard and mouse because he remained thin in spite of eating like a quarterback during training season. If he wasn't hungry, he must not feel well. A bad case of the flu would explain the pallor and dark circles.

"If you're sick, go home. It'll be tough, but I'll get along without you for a day or two."

Dawson stood abruptly, shoving back his chair. "I'm not sick." He strode across the room and out to the main area then sat down beside a bike with an intricate flame design half completed. He picked up a brush and a small pot of paint but didn't open it.

Amanda glanced at Charley who shrugged.

Dawson was always amiable and easy-going.

Amanda looked at the laptop.

"Open it," Charley said. "See what he was doing."

Amanda shook her head. "That wouldn't be right. I can't pry into his business."

She looked at Dawson sitting beside the bike, holding a brush in one hand and a pot of paint in the other, head drooping, gaze seemingly fixed on the floor.

Something was wrong.

She opened the laptop. The screen was blank. She looked at Charley. "Turn it on." In his current condition, Charley's abilities were severely limited, but he was able to influence electronics—turn on the TV in the middle of the night, read Amanda's e-mail when she wasn't looking, set off the alarm system she had installed after Roland Kimball broke into her apartment.

"I hope you remember this the next time you get all upset because I read a few of your e-mails. I'm not the only one who's nosy."

"Just do it, okay?"

He made an elaborate show of waving his hands around and through the laptop as if he were a stage magician performing a trick. Finally he proclaimed, "Ta-da!"

The screen sprang to life.

Charley had told the truth about the display. Numbers and letters in some sort of raw data format. Definitely not a user-friendly Windows program. Why had Dawson been so anxious to hide this? Amanda wouldn't be able to make sense of it if she had the rest of her life to study it.

"He's coming back," Charley warned.

Too late. Dawson stood beside her.

"I'm sorry." Amanda set the laptop back on the desk.

"I'm glad you know." He sank into the chair with an enormous sigh and put his head in his hands. "What should I do?"

Amanda looked from the screen to Dawson to Charley. What was it she was supposed to know from that strange display? If she didn't know what it meant, she certainly didn't know what Dawson should do about it.

"I have no idea what you're talking about. That stuff is gobbledegook to me."

Dawson lifted his head. His glasses sat slightly askew and his eyes had a strange look. The only word that came to mind was *haunted.*

Haunted? Dawson was quiet, intense, OCD, but—*haunted?*

She knelt on the floor in front of him. "You're starting to freak me out. What's going on?"

Dawson clenched his lips and his fists, looking very young and vulnerable, like a child holding in horrible secrets.

Secrets and Dawson didn't go together, but apparently he had a few.

Impossible images raced through Amanda's mind.

Dawson the mild-mannered nerd—a secret life as a bank robber?

Nah.

A spy who sold government secrets?

Certainly not.

A career as a writer of erotica?

Probably not.

He sat straight in the chair, squared his shoulders, and drew in a deep breath. "They took my brother. They're going to kill him if I don't give them a program my dad wrote, and I don't have the program."

Chapter Two

"Your brother?" Amanda frowned. Had she been so obsessed with her own life, with Charley and divorce and murder, she'd somehow missed the fact that Dawson had a brother?

She looked at Charley and mouthed the word, *Brother?*

Charley shrugged. "I never heard of a brother."

She turned her attention back to Dawson and considered how to tactfully bring up her lack of knowledge. "I don't think I ever met your brother, did I?"

Dawson managed a half smile. "No, you've never met him. I never told you about him."

"As I recall, you told me you didn't have a family, that your parents died in an automobile crash."

"They did."

"But you have a brother you sort of forgot to mention? Why? Is he older and lives in another country or up north somewhere?"

"His name is Grant, and he's my little brother. He's eleven years old. We were..." He straightened his glasses and drew in another deep breath. "We were trying to avoid notice. Fly under the radar. But they found us."

Fly under the radar? Dawson had always seemed the epitome of honesty and integrity. What on earth was he talking about? Was he having some sort of paranoid episode? Had he played too many games on the computer? Confused cyberspace with reality? "Who are *they?*"

He shook his head. "I don't know."

Well, at least his mysterious *they* didn't have an identity like Romulans or the CIA. She wasn't sure if that was a good thing or not. "You don't who they are, but you think they took your brother, as in *kidnapped?*"

He nodded.

"Then we need to call the police. Right?"

Dawson shook his head vehemently. "No! They said they'd kill him if I contacted the police!"

Amanda rose slowly to her feet, making an effort to remain calm though her stress level was ratcheting rapidly upward. She gave Charley a desperate look. As a ghost, maybe he had special knowledge of the mysterious *they* who kidnapped boys she'd never heard of and threatened to kill them.

Charley shrugged. "You want my opinion? I think Dawson's lost it."

Amanda didn't often agree with Charley, but she was starting to have some doubts about her assistant. He was not acting rationally. Did he really have a brother? Maybe she hadn't heard about this brother Grant because he didn't exist. Maybe Grant was an avatar in some computer game.

She put her hands on his shoulders. "Dawson, you need to relax. If something's happened to your brother, we'll figure it out. It's going to be all right. I promise." *And if there is no brother and you're flipping out on me, we'll figure that out too.* Dawson was her friend. Friends didn't let friends flip out alone.

Dawson focused on her, blinked twice, and his lips twisted into a wry smile. "You think I'm crazy."

"No, of course not." She dropped her gaze, unable to look at him and lie. "Well, maybe a little."

He turned in the desk chair and pulled out the wide middle drawer.

"He's got a gun!" Charley shouted, dropping to the floor. Heroic as always.

Dawson pulled out a sheet of paper and handed it to Amanda. "I printed the e-mail they sent me last night."

Amanda took the paper tentatively as if it might spin away from her or do something else bizarre.

From: johndoe666@e-mail.com

To: computerguy@e-mail.com

You will receive directions as to when and where to bring your father's source code for Project Verdant. If you fail to do exactly as we tell you, your brother will die. If you contact the police, your brother will die.

Charley came to stand beside her and read the note. "Dawson's playing some kind of a joke."

Amanda looked at the agony on Dawson's face.

It wasn't a joke.

He stood and rolled over another chair. "Sit down," he said. "I need to tell you some things, like my name."

15

Amanda sank into the chair. "Your...name? You're Dawson Page. Aren't you? Of course you are. I checked your references when you came to work here. I made a photocopy of your driver's license. It has your picture. It's you."

Dawson clenched his hands in his lap. "Yeah, about that. It's all a fake. Well, not completely. Dawson is my name. My last name."

Amanda opened her mouth to speak then closed it when she couldn't think of anything to say. That morning the sun had risen in the east, she'd gone to court with her father and Charley's ghost, and her life had seemed quite normal. Now she felt as if she'd fallen down the rabbit hole even though she hadn't had any mushrooms. Not even any cheap champagne.

"What is he trying to hide?" Charley, never at a loss for words, demanded. "Ask him what he's trying to hide. People don't change their names unless they're trying to hide something. You get on my case because I've done a few little things like blackmail and adultery and all the time you've been harboring a mass murderer!"

Little things like blackmail and adultery? Dawson a *mass murderer*? Maybe Charley had been nibbling on a magic mushroom.

"I don't understand. You're a clean cut college kid studying computer science and art. Are you saying that's not who you are?"

"No—I mean, yes, that's who I am. But my real name..." His gaze darted around the room, searching the corners, as if he expected to find someone lurking in the shadows. Romulan? CIA agent? White rabbit?

Even if Dawson's agony was real, Amanda couldn't rule out the possibility that his delusion wasn't.

She leaned forward. "Your *real* name?"

He cleared his throat. "Kevin Dawson. My parents were Wesley and Carol Dawson. Maybe I shouldn't have kept Dawson as part of my name or let Grant keep his real first name. But he was so little and scared. It was bad enough we lost our parents. We both just wanted to keep some part of our family, but maybe that's how they found us." He met Amanda's gaze. "I'm not making any sense, am I?"

That was the first sane thing he'd said since she'd walked in the door. She shook her head slowly. "No. Not really."

He exhaled a long sigh and straightened his shoulders. "My father left us several false identities to choose from. I probably should have chosen one of the others, like John Ferguson or Thomas Waller. It was just so hard to let go of my real name, of all connection to my life and my parents."

"You're still not making sense. Why don't I get fresh Cokes and you start from the beginning, like why your father left you several false identities."

"Be careful, Amanda," Charley warned. "Fathers leave their sons a house or a gold watch or a life insurance policy. They don't leave them false identities. Something's not right."

Amanda went to the small refrigerator in the corner of the room and took out two Cokes. While she had her back turned to Dawson, she whispered to Charley, "Yeah, you know so much about fathers.

You told me yours was an evil dead drug dealer when he's very nice and very alive and coffee is his drug of choice."

"Amanda, you need to let go of the past. That's probably why I'm stuck here, because you won't forgive and forget. It's good that you have a new problem to focus on. I've always known there was something sneaky about Dawson. You can tell a lot about a person by looking at their eyes. He has shifty eyes."

"Stuff it," she whispered.

Holding two Cokes, she went back to the desk. Dawson looked up as she approached, his blue-gray eyes wide and filled with pain. Yeah, you could tell a lot by looking at a person's eyes. Dawson's gaze was innocent while Charley's...but that wasn't fair. She'd once thought Charley's gaze projected mischief and fun. She'd just missed the totally self-centered part of that mischief and fun.

Dawson accepted the soft drink and gulped a large portion of it.

Amanda's cell phone rang. She took it out of her purse and looked at the name. Her mother. Maybe not the last person in the world she wanted to talk to right now, but pretty far down the list. Dawson was either having a meltdown or his brother had been kidnapped by some mysterious *they*. Jenny's baby shower seemed even less important than it had before, and it already ranked alongside washing her car in a thunderstorm.

She silenced the ringer and shoved it back into her purse. "Let's start at the beginning," she said.

"You told me your parents were both dead, killed in a car crash. Is that true?"

Dawson nodded, the movement jerky. "Mom and Dad were murdered two years ago."

Cold fingers traced down Amanda's spine. "*Murdered*? Not killed in a car accident?"

"They died in a car crash, but it was no accident. It was murder."

The cold fingers raced back up Amanda's spine then clutched around her heart. "Murder?" she repeated.

Charley placed himself between her and Dawson. "You see? He murdered his parents! I told you so! No telling how many other people he's killed!" He balled his fist and threw a punch to and through Dawson's nose.

Dawson shivered. Charley's touch had that effect on people. "Did you turn the air conditioning down?"

"No. It just seems cool in here because it's so hot outside. Texas in July." She brushed a hand through Charley, feeling a chill as she did so. "There's an ugly draft right here."

Dawson reached a hand through Charley's abdomen. "Yeah, there is," he said. "A cold spot. I've never noticed that before."

"I can take a hint." Charley stepped aside. "But I'll be here to protect you when you need me."

The idea of Charley protecting her was such an absurd statement, Amanda fought the urge to laugh. Laughter was not appropriate in the face of murder, kidnapping and possible insanity. "Dawson, tell me about your parents."

"I might as well." He sighed. "There's no reason to hide anything anymore. They've found us and they've got Grant. I've got to save him. I can't let them hurt him. I'm his big brother. Since our parents died, he's looked up to me and expected me to take care of him. I've always tried but now I don't know what to do." He leaned back, his expression bleak as if all hope was gone from the world. From his world.

"They," Amanda repeated. "*They* would be johndoe666@e-mail.com?"

Dawson clutched his Coke can so tightly the sides dented. "I don't know who that is and I don't know what Project Verdant is. I tried to trace the e-mail, but they've bounced it all over the world. When you came in, I was looking at the metadata, but these guys obviously know their way around computers."

That narrowed the field to a few billion people. "Okay, let's get back to your parents. Tell me why you think their deaths were murder and not an accident."

"The police said so. I guess I need to tell you the whole story."

"Yes," Amanda agreed, "you do. The whole story would be a good place to start."

"We lived in Kansas City. My dad was a professor at a university in Kansas. He taught economics, but his passion was computers. He had me coding while I was still in grade school." Dawson's lips tilted upward in a small sad smile at the memory.

"Coding?" Amanda repeated. "Like in *The DaVinci Code*?" Instead of clearing things up, Dawson sounded goofier with every word.

"Writing source code for computer programs. You write it in English, then you compile it to machine language and—"

Amanda held up a hand. She could tell Dawson was going off into a language that might as well be machine code for all it meant to her. He did that a lot, assumed she understood everything he said. "Got it. You were writing computer programs at an early age. Go on."

"Mom worked at a bank. She taught college before Grant and I came along, but she liked the short hours at the bank so she could spend more time with us."

"They sound like wonderful people. I'm sorry you lost them so young."

Charley snorted. "I can't believe you're really falling for this garbage."

Amanda made a note to remind Charley that she'd been naïve enough to fall for his garbage and marry him.

"My parents were wonderful," Dawson agreed. "Looking back, I think they got a little quiet and secretive in the last few months of their lives, but I didn't really notice at the time. I was only eighteen. I'd just graduated from high school and was excited about going on to college. I was a selfish kid, completely involved in my own life."

He sounded as if he thought eighteen was very young and very long ago, but if his parents died two years before, he could only be twenty now. Three years younger than the identification he'd given her when he applied for the job as her assistant. Then or now, one time or the other, he'd deceived her. She'd have sworn he was always honest, incapable of deceit. Second time she'd got that wrong about somebody, and the first one still haunted her. Literally.

"One evening Mom and Dad went to a play. Grant and I were supposed to go too. We had season tickets for all of us, and usually we went together. But that night Grant wanted to stay home and play some online game with his buddies. I made fun of him for wanting to play a little kid game." Dawson bit his lip. "I didn't mean it. I was just being a rude big brother. But I told Mom and Dad I'd stay home with him. The play was a musical, and I didn't really want to go either. So they went without us, and on the way home, their car ran off the road and crashed. There wasn't a lot left of the car, but the police found evidence of a bomb."

Amanda's hand flew to her mouth. "Oh, Dawson! I'm so sorry!" She still wasn't sure about the false identities and the kidnapped brother, but she heard the sincerity and sadness in his voice when he spoke of his parents' deaths.

Charley harrumphed.

"The police came to the door and told us. They offered to send over a counselor, but Grant and I didn't want a stranger in the house. Grant kept saying it wasn't true, they'd made a mistake. He was nine then, just a little kid. He ran into their room and started throwing things around, looking everywhere, like he was going to find them in the closet or under the bed. I tried to calm him, but then he opened Dad's briefcase, and there was an envelope addressed to Mom that said, *To be opened in the event of my death.*" He paused and swallowed. "I opened it and found a key to a safe deposit box along with a letter telling her what to do if anything happened to him. In that letter he said he was talking to the authorities, but he wasn't sure he trusted the guy. He said the safe deposit box contained cash and new identities for Mom, Grant and me in case something happened. I guess he hadn't counted on Mom being killed too."

Dawson lifted his glasses and blotted the corners of his eyes with one finger.

"In his letter Dad gave instructions that we should pack what we could get in the car, put my bicycle on the rack, drive north and abandon the car in Nebraska. I was then to take the bicycle and ride to a used car lot. With one of the new identities, I was to buy another car for cash. We were to take that car and head south to Texas. If we ever felt threatened, we were to pick up and move again using another identity. Grant and I were freaked out that our parents were dead, and we didn't know what to do. So we did what he said. We ran."

"I don't understand," Amanda said slowly, trying to take in the strange tale. "What was your father talking to the authorities about? Who are you running from?" The mysterious *they* again?

Dawson pulled off his glasses and shook his head. "I don't know. That's the problem. I assume

Mom knew, but she's dead too. Now these people want some code that Dad wrote for Project Verdant, and I don't have it. I took all our laptops when we ran, Dad's, mine and Grant's. I know about computers. I've been through all of them, and I can't find anything about Project Verdant. There's a lot of code that Dad wrote, but it's all small stuff for his economics classes. I can't give them what I don't have. How am I going to get my brother back?"

Amanda shivered. If Dawson was telling the truth, if he was sane and sober, the situation was bad. If he wasn't...either way, they were in trouble.

Chapter Three

Dawson picked up the laptop and rose. "I'm sorry. I can't work today. I need to go home and..." He shrugged. "I don't know. Search through the computers again. Do something."

Though he stood only a couple of feet away, Dawson seemed to be a million miles away, all alone and scared. Amanda thought of her own recent trip to the courthouse with her father by her side. She could have done it without him, but it had meant a lot to have him with her. Later in the day she would be meeting her birth mother for a celebration. Then there was also the mother who'd raised her and wanted to see her, albeit to talk about baby shower invitations. Her family might be a little offbeat, but they were there for her. Dawson was facing his problem alone.

"Of course you can't work today. Neither can I. We're not busy. We'll close the place and I'll go with you to your apartment to help you look for Grant." Or look for his sanity. Whichever had been lost.

Dawson shook his head. "I appreciate that, but there's nothing you can do. My brother's gone. They came in and took him in the middle of the night and didn't leave any trace evidence."

"Trace evidence?" Charley repeated. "He's been watching too many crime shows. Do not go with him to his apartment. He'll get you in there and lop off your head."

"I'm sure you know more about trace evidence than I do." Amanda spoke to Dawson while glaring at Charley. "But let's go look again anyway. We'll start at the last place you saw your brother. Where and when was that?" If he said he'd last seen his brother during a computer game, she wouldn't count on finding any unknown DNA in his apartment.

"Last night. He finished his homework, went into his bedroom and closed the door, and that's the last time I saw him. I didn't even check on him. I just left him in there, and they took him." Dawson headed for the door, his movements mechanical like those of a robot.

This man should not be allowed to ride the motorcycle that was his only mode of transportation. That settled it. She absolutely had to go with him, help him somehow.

"We should take the truck," she said, referring to the battered pick-up they used to transport bikes and parts. "Leave your bike here. I'll drive."

Dawson looked back, his expression vague. "Okay."

He hated to ride in that truck with its disorderly ripped seats, missing radio knobs and other imperfections. It completely offended his OCD sense of order. The fact that he didn't argue about riding in the truck or leaving his bike at the shop said a lot about how upset he was.

"I'm going too. You shouldn't be alone with him." Charley made it sound as if he had a choice of whether or not to go along when the reality was that he couldn't get more than a few hundred feet away from her. They were bound by some invisible tether which neither seemed able to break. When she'd filed for divorce while he was still alive, he'd told her he was never going to let her go. It appeared for once he hadn't lied. "I'll ride in the back of the truck," he said. "You might want to think about riding back there too just in case Dawson loses it and attacks you with a thumb drive or a CD or something."

Amanda shot him an irritated glance. Whether or not Dawson really had a brother, he was suffering. Charley had not been a compassionate person when he was alive, and dying had improved him only marginally. Amanda could understand why that white light had been snatched away from him, and he didn't seem to be making much progress toward reaching it.

ॐॐ

As Dawson directed Amanda to his apartment building, she realized she had only a vague idea of where he lived. In their two year association, he had kept secrets, and she'd been so involved in her own problems, she'd never even noticed.

A few miles from her office, they pulled up to a run-down red brick apartment building. Their dilapidated truck fit right in with the other vehicles in the small, badly maintained parking lot behind the building.

Amanda, Dawson, and Charley went around the side of the building and along the cracked walk to the front door.

"This place sucks," Charley said. "You need to pay crazy boy more money."

Too bad Charley was already dead. Amanda would like to kill him herself or at least torture him for a few hours. She hadn't figured out a way to torture a ghost but she hadn't given up on the idea.

They walked inside the building and were greeted with the smells of moldy carpet and stale cigarette smoke. Maybe she *should* be paying Dawson more.

Wordlessly he moved to the staircase and started to climb.

Amanda followed.

"I'll take the elevator." Charley shot upward, laughing.

Since he was only energy in his current state, maybe she could zap him with a battery charger and cause an overload. Or suck him into a rechargeable battery then put that battery in a flashlight and leave it on until the charge was exhausted.

Upon reaching the third floor, Dawson led her to a door marked 3D in black metal digits. He unlocked two deadbolts and opened the door.

The apartment was old but immaculate. No surprise there. Dawson regularly created order from her chaos at the shop. The furniture was minimal with little of a personal nature. No paintings decorated the walls, no vases or candles sat on the dust-free coffee table, no sign that people lived there.

Dawson set the laptop on a small kitchen table off to one side of the living room. Two more laptops were already on the table. Dawson had mentioned three laptops...his, Grant's and their father's. One checkmark in the sanity column.

"Where's Grant's bedroom?" she asked.

"Over here." Dawson crossed the faded but clean tan carpet to a short hallway and opened the first door.

The change was radical. Dallas Cowboys and Texas Rangers posters covered the walls. An MP3 player with headphones sat on the small desk. Rumpled sheets and a colorful spread draped half on and half off the twin size bed. An eleven year old boy could live in this room, an eleven year old boy who'd been taken from that very bed during the night. Dawson's story was becoming more credible.

He walked over to the bed and picked up a stuffed dog that was missing one ear, most of his hair and some of his stuffing. "Mom and Dad gave him this for his fourth birthday. He'd already stopped sleeping with it before they died. He said he was too big to play with stuffed animals, but he brought it when we had to leave and now he sleeps with it every night." He turned pain-filled eyes toward Amanda. "We have to get him back. He can't sleep tonight without his dog."

"Do you have a picture of your brother?"

He nodded and left the room. Amanda stood in the doorway of the child's room, afraid to enter for fear she might destroy some of that *trace evidence* Dawson hadn't been able to find.

Charley had no such inhibitions. He darted in and reached down as if to touch the bed, but his hand slid into it.

"Don't do that," Amanda protested. "You might contaminate...oh, never mind. I guess a ghost can't contaminate evidence."

Charley flinched. "I hate it when you do that, call me a ghost and act like I don't matter."

Dawson returned with a framed picture and handed it to her. Amanda studied the family looking back at her, four happy people smiling at an unseen camera. An older version of Dawson stood with his arm draped around an attractive woman with kind eyes. Dawson, a couple of years younger and wearing a carefree smile she'd never seen, sat next to a boy with a mischievous grin. Grant?

"It's a few years old." Dawson touched the boy's image. "We didn't take pictures after Mom and Dad died. I guess I should have, but I never thought about it."

Dawson had a brother. Pictures didn't lie.

Amanda's gaze moved from his haggard face to the empty bed. More evidence that his story was true, that his brother had been kidnapped. But if she believed him, she had to believe the whole incredible story about the false identities, hiding from mysterious murderers and trying to find hidden source code. "We've got to call the police," she said decisively. "Detective Jake Daggett, the guy who helped take down Roland Kimball, he can help us."

"No! Not the police! They said not to call the police! They killed my parents. They'll kill my brother."

"We can ask Daggett to keep it quiet. We can trust him."

"No!" Charley protested even more vehemently than Dawson. "You can't trust that damned Daggett."

Amanda arched a questioning eyebrow at him.

"He's...he's a cowboy. He could get you killed. Remember how he acted in Silver Creek."

Amanda remembered that Daggett had charged in at the eleventh hour to capture Roland Kimball, and she and Daggett had subsequently spent some time together as she went through the process of giving her statements so they could convict the evil man. Charley had no reason to call him a cowboy except that he was good looking and rugged in a Texas cowboy sort of way.

And that probably explained why Charley didn't want Detective Daggett around. Jealousy of something he'd never been.

Dawson turned away and ran a hand through his hair, making it even messier. "We don't dare call in the police. I've got to find that source code and give it to those people." He threw his hands out in a gesture of helplessness. "But I don't know where else to look. I have no idea what Project Verdant is. Verdant means green. A green project? Recycling? Solar energy? There's nothing like that in any of Dad's programs."

"Okay, okay!" Amanda moved to him and took his hands in hers. She could barely manage her own life, but somehow she had to take control of the situation, calm Dawson, figure out what to do next. She knew how to repair motorcycles, open a can of Coke and call for pizza delivery, but she had no idea how to soothe her frantic friend or how to locate a missing boy.

"Dawson, you're the smartest person I know. You need to relax and think. We can do this."

He grabbed onto her hands as if grabbing a lifeline, his desperate expression suddenly hopeful.

Damn. He was counting on her and she had no idea what to do.

When all else fails and your mind goes completely blank, fall back on manners.

It was Texas, and a stressful situation called for a hot beverage even though it was at least ninety degrees outside.

"Do you have tea or hot chocolate?"

Dawson nodded.

"Let's make something to drink and talk this through. Where's your tea and where are your cups?"

He led her back to the living room and indicated the small kitchen separated by an open bar. "In the cabinet."

Amanda didn't ask which cabinet. There were only a couple to choose from. She'd find what she needed.

She located two thick white mugs, filled them with water and turned around once then twice. No microwave. She was definitely going to have to redo her budget and figure out a way to pay him more. How on earth did he cook frozen dinners without a microwave?

She found a pan, poured in the water and heated it on the small stove, then cringed when she found the tea—store brand tea bags. Well, it would have to do.

She poured the hot water into the cups, added tea bags, and took them to the table in the dining area.

"I might like to have a cup of tea too," Charley complained. "But no, just ignore the ghost."

"Do you have a notepad and pen?" Amanda asked Dawson, trying her best to ignore the ghost.

He brought the requested items to the table.

Charley sat on the chair in front of Amanda's cup of tea and grinned at her when she approached. "Come sit on my lap."

Amanda took another chair and moved her cup over. "You write," she said when Dawson shoved the paper toward her. "Can't read my own writing once it gets cold." She took a drink of the store brand tea and tried not to grimace. "First we need to search through everything you brought with you when you left your old house."

"We didn't bring a lot, just what we could throw in the car, and I've already been through all of it three times searching for something—an external hard drive, a flash drive, a CD, even a printout, anything that might contain source code. I haven't found anything."

Dawson could spot a 6-32 set screw in a bin full of fasteners from across a tool crib, so if he hadn't found anything, there probably was nothing to find. But she couldn't say that, couldn't let him accept defeat. "I haven't been through it. Fresh eyes. Write that down. Number one, search possessions for something that could contain source code."

Dawson dutifully wrote on the notepad in his meticulous penmanship. He'd probably never had a teacher tell him he was going to get a C in penmanship because all his other grades were As, but he actually deserved an F for such terrible handwriting. Not that Amanda's bad handwriting bothered her. That was why God invented word processing programs.

Dawson finished writing and looked at her, waiting.

Amanda took another sip of tea, trying to think of what to say next. "What about the rest of it, the stuff you didn't bring, the stuff you left in Kansas City?"

"The mortgage company foreclosed on the house and set the furniture and everything out on the sidewalk for strangers to take."

Amanda flinched at the image. "Are you sure? How do you know when you're down here and the house is up there?"

"Internet."

"Oh." She drew in a deep breath. "If that program was still somewhere in the house..." She bit off the sentence as she realized what she was about to say. The unspoken conclusion hung in the air between them.

Charley frowned. "If it was in the house, it's gone and he can't give it to the kidnappers which means they'll kill his brother. Oh. I see. You knew that, didn't you?"

Dawson's features crumpled and for a moment Amanda thought he was going to cry. He took off his glasses and wiped his eyes then put them back on.

"So we will find your brother," she blurted, then wondered if it was possible the absurd statement had come from her own lips. How did she expect to find a kidnapped child?

"Really, Sherlock Holmes?" Charley jeered. "And just how do you think you're going to do that?"

"How?" Dawson echoed Charley's question. However, unlike Charley, he still had the hopeful expression that made her cringe inside and swear a personal vow that she would somehow find Grant.

"Keep writing. Two." Amanda gestured at the notepad.

Dawson ducked his head and dutifully wrote "*2*" on the pad.

Amanda took another sip of the bitter tea, buying time while she decided what on earth she was going to say next.

"Two. Search Grant's room for, uh, trace evidence."

"I've already done that."

"But I haven't. Fresh eyes." She was trying to find suggestions to make Dawson feel better. She had no intention of searching Grant's room in case there was something the police could use when Dawson finally agreed they had to call them in. "Write it down."

"This is crazy, Amanda!" Charley leaned through the table toward her. "You have no idea what trace evidence looks like, and you wouldn't know what to do with it if you found it. You need to call the cops, just not that Daggett guy. They can either find the missing kid if there is one or get Dawson committed if there isn't. Maybe he murdered his little brother and hid the body and this is his cover story."

Ignoring Charley, Amanda watched Dawson write her words then look at her expectantly.

"Three." She tried to remember what they did on TV shows when they were looking for a missing person. "We talk to your neighbors." Actually, that didn't sound like a bad idea, the only good one she'd come up with yet. "And we'll do *three* before *one* and *two* since you already did *one* and *two*."

Dawson frowned then started to tear off the top sheet.

"Stop. You don't need to start all over and change the numbers." The boy was definitely OCD.

Fear joined the anguish in his eyes. "I don't know my neighbors. I've avoided them ever since we've been here."

"I know, fly under the radar. No problem. I'll talk to them." She pushed back her chair and stood.

Dawson followed her example, squaring his shoulders. "I'll go with you. I guess it's too late to hide."

They went back out into the hallway with its stained green carpet and rancid smells. Three more apartments besides Dawson's on that floor. Twelve apartments in all. Surely a boy couldn't disappear from the building without somebody seeing something.

She turned to Dawson. "You don't know who lives next door to you?" She indicated the apartment beside his, 3C.

He shook his head. "I know there are two women on the other side of me, but I don't know anything about this apartment or the one next to it. Sometimes I hear strange noises coming from this one."

"Strange noises? Like what?"

"Electronic noises. Beeps, buzzing."

"Chainsaws," Charley said. "Chopping people up. I don't think you should go in there."

That image did not make her feel even a little bit better about this visit. "Okay, let's go talk to whoever lives in 3C."

Amanda knocked on the scarred wooden door.

"I'll just pop in and see if he's got the brother and if the kid's still alive. If he has a chainsaw, you probably shouldn't disturb him." Charley disappeared through the door.

No one responded to her knock. No sounds came from inside. "Whoever lives here is probably at work." Amanda knocked again.

Charley darted through the door, back into the hallway, looking as if he'd seen a ghost.

"He's home all right! You are not going to freaking believe this!"

Chapter Four

Amanda gasped and jumped backward, away from the door, as images of a torture chamber with chains, saws and several dead bodies flashed through her mind.

"What's wrong?" Panic edged Dawson's words "What did you hear? Is Grant in there? Are they hurting him?"

The door opened a crack.

Amanda turned to run but bumped into Dawson. He shoved her aside and pushed against the door, almost knocking over a short man wearing a tinfoil hat, thick glasses and an annoyed expression. "Who are you? What do you want?"

"I'm your neighbor." Dawson's voice was surprisingly firm. Concern for his brother had emboldened his normally reticent nature.

His courage made Amanda braver. "We need to talk to you." She glanced at Charley to see if he was going to protest, warn them away from whatever he'd seen inside.

"You gotta see this," Charley said.

Amanda shuddered and sent up a silent prayer that he wouldn't think she needed to see a torture chamber or mutilated bodies. "Can we come in?"

The young man looked at her, shrugged, causing his shiny hat to tilt precariously, and opened the door wider to allow them entrance.

For once Charley had neither lied nor exaggerated. If Amanda had not seen it for herself, she would not have freaking believed it.

The walls and windows were covered with tinfoil. The furniture consisted of four long tables holding monitors, computer towers, laptops, and other machines Amanda couldn't readily identify. Pieces of tinfoil in various sizes and shapes lay on or beside most of the machines. Electric cords and wires draped the tables and ran along the floor like Christmas tinsel on steroids.

"Come in," the neighbor invited then darted back into the room and began shoving magazines off two wooden chairs.

Dawson strode in without hesitation.

"It's like that in the kitchen and bedroom too." Charley smiled proudly as if he were somehow responsible for the unique décor.

"Is Grant here?" Amanda whispered, inclining her head toward the open door to the bedroom.

Charley shook his head. "No, just more aluminum foil. Guy must have hit one heck of a sale."

Marginally reassured that, while the man might be a kook, he wasn't a homicidal kook, Amanda moved inside and took a seat on the chair next to Dawson.

The kook closed the door behind her then rolled an office chair away from one of the tables and settled onto it. "So you're my neighbors." He studied Dawson and Amanda with pale, watery eyes magnified ridiculously by the thick lenses. Those glasses had to be twenty years old, a relic from an era before the invention of ultrathin lenses.

"He's your neighbor." Amanda indicated Dawson. "He's Dawson Page. I'm Amanda Caulfield."

The kook nodded. "Yes, yes, I've seen him leaving his apartment. I'm Brendan Matthews. What did you want to talk to me about?"

"You're not with the police department, are you?" Dawson asked cautiously.

Matthews jerked his head around as if the spoken word might make the police materialize. "No, I am most certainly not allied with those government spies."

"Good, that's good."

Matthews' attitude didn't sound at all good to Amanda. He sounded like a total nut job. But at least Dawson would be willing to talk to him if he wasn't a cop. "Dawson's little brother is missing, and we just wondered if you might have seen anything."

Matthews scowled. "Anything? I've seen a lot."

"Have you seen somebody hustling a little boy out of the building, a stranger lurking around the building, somebody you haven't seen before?" Amanda didn't expect much from this guy. He would have to have x-ray vision to see through all the foil, but he had recognized Dawson so it was possible he knew something.

"What does he look like, this little brother?"

40

"Grant is eleven years old. He's four and a half feet tall, weighs seventy-two pounds. He's a little thin because he's always running around doing something, playing baseball, riding his bicycle..." Dawson bit off his words, licked his lips and started again. "He has brown hair and blue eyes. Have you seen him?"

Matthews shook his head and frowned. "I didn't know you had a brother. I've seen you coming and going, but never a child. Has this child always been with you or did he come here recently?"

Dawson leaned forward, his posture rigid and urgent. "He's always been with me. We've lived in that apartment for two years. He rides his bicycle to school every day. One day he fell on the sidewalk and skinned his knee right in front of this building. You must have seen him!" As if he suddenly realized he was becoming hysterical, Dawson sat back and drew a shaky hand over his face.

Ice wrapped around Amanda's heart. Again the question had arisen of whether Grant was real or not. Dawson had the photograph and the little boy's room. Grant had existed. But she had no proof he was still alive. Maybe he'd died in the car wreck that killed their parents. Maybe Dawson was suffering from an emotional trauma. Maybe—

"*They* took him."

Amanda gasped in shock at Matthews' words, the same ones Dawson had spoken earlier.

Dawson shot to his feet and stood looming over Matthews who remained sitting. "What do you know about them?" Dawson demanded. "Where did they take Grant?"

Matthews shook his head, causing his strange hat to tremble. "You didn't have any protection, did you?"

"Protection?" Amanda echoed. Surely he wasn't talking about condoms. "You mean like a gun?"

Matthews snorted. "You couldn't stop them with a regular gun."

This conversation was getting weirder and weirder. "I'm pretty sure I could stop anybody but Superman with my .38, especially since it's loaded with jacketed hollow points."

Matthews snorted again, more vehemently this time. "You couldn't even stop a Venusian with a .38, and the ones from Alpha Centauri have diamond based skin. Don't waste your bullets. You need a laser gun."

Amanda's chin dropped. Charley had even been stricken dumb. Dawson had rambled on about a mysterious *they*, but Brendan Matthews was more specific—Venusians and creatures from Alpha Centauri.

Dawson blinked a couple of times, stepped back and stared at the man in the tinfoil hat. "Alpha Centauri? Diamond based skin?"

"Yes, they're the ones who've been skulking around lately. They're the ones who took your brother."

"That guy is seriously nuts!" Charley moved toward the door as if fearful that proximity to Matthews would infect him with the *seriously nuts* virus. Too late. Charley had been seriously nuts as long as she'd known him.

"Thank you so much for talking to us, Mr. Matthews. Dawson, I think I hear the phone in your apartment ringing. We need to go."

She grabbed Dawson's arm and dragged him toward the door before he could protest that he didn't have a landline.

"I have some extra foil," Matthews offered. "And I can help you set up the shield program on your computer."

"Thank you, we'll get back to you on that." Amanda opened the door with one hand and pushed Dawson through with the other.

The dreariness of the hallway was a welcome change from the shiny insanity of apartment 3C. Amanda drew in a deep breath of the stale air.

Dawson took two steps forward then two back and shook his head. "What was that man talking about? Is he saying aliens took Grant?"

"Yeah, I think that's what he was saying." Dawson was close to losing it, dependent on her to hold him together. She wasn't cut out for that job. She was way more familiar with being the panicker than the soother. But she had to help her friend. "Okay, you got a kooky neighbor. It happens. Let's go talk to your other neighbors. Who knows? One of them may actually be from Alpha Centauri. I think that's probably where Charley came from."

That got a half-smile from Dawson. "No, he didn't have diamond based skin."

"Not funny, Amanda." Charley floated ahead of them down the hall and disappeared into apartment 3B.

A loud scream burst from the apartment.

Amanda and Dawson exchanged a horrified look then dashed toward the door.

Charley slid back out, looking frazzled. "Cat. I guess he could see me. Guy's another nut job. No sign of a kidnapped kid."

Another nut job? Was the building a refuge for tin foil freaks?

Dawson pounded on the door. "Open up!"

The door opened almost immediately to reveal a tall well-muscled man in a tight T-shirt and workout pants. He didn't look like a nut. He looked pretty good, actually.

Dawson lunged toward him. Amanda grabbed Dawson around the waist in a futile effort to hold him back. "It was a cat, not your brother!"

The man reacted defensively, grabbing Dawson's arm and twisting it behind his back. "Who are you?" he demanded. "What the hell's going on?"

A Siamese cat darted into the hall, looked up at Charley, hissed and shrieked in a voice at least ten times his size.

Dawson ceased struggling and looked at the spitting, screaming animal. "A cat?"

"A cat."

He lifted his gaze to the man who held him in his grip. "I'm sorry. I thought..."

Amanda stepped forward and offered her hand. "Hi. I'm Amanda Caulfield and this is Dawson Page.

He lives in apartment 3D, and he doesn't usually attack people. We heard your cat and thought it was a person, Dawson's brother, to be exact."

The man studied her for a moment then released Dawson and shook her hand. "I'm Nick Farner. Yeah, Miss Kitty gets pretty loud sometimes. I have no idea what's got her so upset this time." He stepped around Dawson and picked up the cat who continued to grumble at Charley.

"I know how you feel, Miss Kitty." Amanda tentatively stroked the cat's head. "I'm sorry about the misunderstanding, Mr. Farner. Dawson's brother is missing, and he's very upset. We'd really appreciate it if you could take a few minutes to talk to us." She gave him the sweet smile her mother had tried for years to get her to use. It didn't come naturally, but this was a desperate time.

Nick looked from her to Dawson then finally shrugged and stepped back, holding the door open. "Come on in."

Behind him Amanda could see an apartment furnished with shabby but elegant antiques.

Amanda arched a questioning eyebrow at Charley as she and Dawson entered the apartment. She and Charley obviously had a very different idea of what constituted a *nut job*. He'd been right about Brendan Matthews, but Nick Farner seemed pretty normal.

Charley kept close to her side, as far away from Nick and the cat as he could get. "Yeah, I stand by what I said. Another nut job. What normal guy would live in an apartment like this? It reminds me of your grandmother's house. Your first grandmother. Well, I guess she was actually your second grandmother. But the first one you knew about. The one with the big house in Highland Park. You have too many mothers and that makes for way too many grandmothers."

Amanda moved past him and sat on the faded damask sofa. Dawson sat tentatively beside her, tense as if he still didn't quite trust this man.

Nick Farner closed the door, put the cat in the bedroom and took a seat in the matching arm chair. His virility did look a little out of place in the faded rose colored Victorian style chair. "So what's going on?"

"Are you with the police?" Dawson blurted.

Farner studied him a long moment as if not quite sure how to take the strange question. "No, I'm a personal trainer. Why would think I'm with the police?"

Amanda chose to avoid the question rather than answer it. "Dawson's little brother is missing. We just thought you might have seen something, maybe noticed a stranger hanging around."

"What does your brother look like? I don't think I've ever seen him. I've seen you going in and out, but I never saw you with a little boy."

Another neighbor who hadn't seen Grant. Another question as to whether Grant existed.

"He lives with me." Dawson's voice was becoming edgy.

Maybe this interview business wasn't such a good idea.

"Have you seen anybody around here who looked suspicious, somebody who doesn't belong?" Amanda asked. "Somebody you haven't seen before?"

Nick leaned forward and studied his two visitors carefully. "If your little brother is missing, you should call the police."

"No, we can't do that." Dawson clasped his hands in his lap.

"We, uh, think maybe he went off with a friend and he's, uh, trying to get back at Dawson for grounding him by disappearing. It would be very embarrassing if we called the cops and then he came home."

"You're getting pretty good at this lying business," Charley said approvingly, settling beside her on the sofa...a couple of inches above the sofa.

Farner looked dubious, and Amanda suspected she was not nearly as proficient a liar as Charley. Not that she aspired to that skill, but it would be handy in the current situation.

"I wish I could help you," Farner said, "but I don't recall seeing the boy or anybody suspicious, anybody who looked out of place."

Amanda rose with a sigh. "Thank you for talking to us. If you do see something, please let us know."

Farner stood. "I will. I hope your brother comes home soon. I ran away once when I was a kid. I had no idea what torment I was putting my parents through. Don't be too hard on your brother when he finally shows up." He smiled and held the door open.

Back outside in the dreary hallway Amanda sighed. "Well, at least this neighbor was normal, but we still didn't learn anything."

Dawson frowned and looked at the closed door of 3B. "Something's not right."

"Really? We just came from the apartment of a man who sees visitors from another star system, but you think there's something not right about this guy with big shoulders and antique furniture?"

Dawson lifted a hand to his forehead. "There's something about him that bothers me."

"What?"

"I don't know. I'm just stressed, I guess."

"That's understandable. We're not getting anywhere. We'll talk to the people in the last apartment on this floor and then we need to go to Plan B."

"What's Plan B?"

Call the police. She refrained from saying it aloud.

"Let's go check on the ladies in 3A. You did say two women, didn't you? Interesting that you noticed the women but not the guys," she teased.

Dawson managed a strained smile. "I'd have remembered the guy in tinfoil if I'd ever seen him. I think he stays inside his apartment and communicates with aliens."

Amanda nodded. "You're probably right. Okay, on to 3A."

"The girls may be gone right now. I've passed them in the mornings on their way out of the building. They usually have books with them. College students, I think."

Amanda strode over to the door marked 3A and knocked. No one answered.

Charley darted in then came back shortly. "Nobody home. No tinfoil. No old furniture. Looks like a normal place."

"Okay, we'll check with them later," Amanda said.

"Do you want to try the people on the first and second floors?" Dawson asked. "Maybe by then the girls will have come home."

Not that the girls were likely to know anything either. It was time to resort to Plan B. "Let's go back into your apartment and talk."

Dawson hesitated, looking around as if searching for something they'd missed. Finally he sighed and opened the door of his own apartment.

They sat again at the table with the cups of cooling store brand tea. Amanda wasn't about to drink any more of it, but she wrapped her hands around the mug. It was something to do.

"We're getting nowhere," she said. "We don't know what we're doing."

Dawson drew in a shaky breath. "I realize that."

"We need help, somebody who has experience at this sort of thing. We've got to call the police."

"No!"

"Yes. They'll know what to do. We'll call Detective Daggett and he'll be able to make sure nobody finds out we've talked to them."

"No!" Charley echoed Dawson's refusal. For emphasis he darted up to the ceiling then back down again, half through the table, his face a few inches from Amanda's as he scowled at her. "That's not a good idea."

"We'll swear him to secrecy," she promised, trying unsuccessfully to lean around Charley who matched her every movement. To Dawson who couldn't see Charley, she probably looked like a drunken snake charmer swaying back and forth. "I'm sure they've dealt with this sort of thing before. Daggett will be able to help. Remember when we were trying to catch Kimball, Jake Daggett was so secretive he didn't even tell me he was working on my case."

"The people who have Grant are computer literate. Maybe they can even hack into the police computers."

"Then we'll tell Daggett not to enter anything into the computer. He always carries a little notebook that he writes stuff in. Anyway, we don't have a choice," Amanda said firmly. "Your brother's in trouble and we don't have the ability to help him. He's counting on his big brother. We can't let him down."

Dawson sagged in his chair. He swallowed hard then gave a brief nod. "Tell Daggett that Grant's life is in danger if those people find out we've talked to him."

"I will." Amanda took her cell phone from her purse. Jake Daggett would know what to do. And he'd have the resources to find out if little brother

Grant had died in the car wreck that killed Dawson's parents. She didn't want to think that Dawson could be mentally ill, but the two neighbors they'd talked to had never seen the boy, and the story he'd told about false identities and running from unknown killers was pretty far-fetched.

Of course, having her ex-husband's ghost hanging around was a little far-fetched too.

Chapter Five

Half an hour and two cups of bad tea later, a knock sounded on Dawson's front door. He darted an anxious glance in that direction and Charley swept through the door then back again.

"It's that cop," he reported, a disgusted look on his face. "Brought a buddy with him. Just what we need. Two of them."

Amanda thought they could probably use the entire Dallas Police Department, but two was a good start. "It's Daggett," she said to reassure Dawson before she went to the door and opened it.

She hadn't seen Detective Jake Daggett for a couple of weeks, not since they'd finally concluded all the details of locking away Roland Kimball. The man looked good in a disheveled sort of way with his piercing brown eyes, dark hair that always seemed to be two weeks overdue for a haircut and cop muscles that stretched his T-shirt nicely. For a fleeting instant she admitted to herself that perhaps Charley's jealousy of the guy had some merit.

But that was silly. She was glad to see Jake because he could help Dawson. Nothing more.

She didn't recognize the other guy, but he had that same indefinable air of being a cop. He also filled out his T-shirt with more than adequate muscles. Cops must spend a lot of time at the gym.

Both men wore faded jeans and scuffed cowboy boots. The new guy was more clean cut with short black hair and a definite Italian look. He carried a backpack that appeared to be stuffed full of something. Doubtless more cop stuff.

Amanda could only hope their cop aura wasn't as obvious to anyone who might be observing as it was to her.

Impulsively she stepped forward, reached up and wrapped her arms around Jake's neck. "Good to see you again, *cousin Jake*," she said loudly, then whispered, "Play along in case the kidnappers are watching so they won't think you're cops."

"Hey!" Charley protested. "You don't need to do that!"

She probably didn't need to, but it seemed like a good idea.

Jake hugged her back. "Good to see you too, *cousin Amanda*." He returned her hug enthusiastically enough to convince any possible eavesdropping kidnappers that they were personally involved.

"Okay, Amanda, that's enough," Charley said. "We've got a crime to solve."

Maybe the embrace had lasted a few seconds longer than necessary. Of course, that all depended on the definition of *necessary*. Amanda hadn't minded.

Both men came inside and she closed the door behind them. "Jake, you remember my assistant, Dawson Page."

Jake nodded to Dawson then indicated his buddy. "This is Detective Ross Minatelli. He's a forensics specialist."

The second detective smiled, faint lines crinkling around bright brown eyes, white teeth sparkling against olive skin. Except for the cop aura, he seemed like a perfectly charming guy. He extended a hand and Amanda shook it. "Pleased to meet you, ma'am."

Dawson stepped forward, his movements jerky, his face pale. "You told someone else?" he accused Jake. "They told me not to contact the police. I didn't even want Amanda to call you, but I trusted you, and now you've brought in a stranger?"

"It's okay," Jake assured him. "Ross has worked kidnappings before. He knows the drill, and I need his expertise. Let's sit down and talk about this." He pulled out his perennial pen and notebook and moved toward the table.

"Where did you park?" Dawson asked. "Did you come in a squad car? What if they're watching?"

"We came in an old Ford with plates that will show up as *not on file* if anybody checks. Don't worry. We know what we're doing. This is not our first kidnapping."

Dawson let out a long breath and stepped back. "Okay. I'm sorry. Amanda's right. We need help finding my brother. Thank you for coming."

"Would you like some tea?" Amanda offered.

"Or coffee. I have coffee. Amanda doesn't like coffee, but I have some." Dawson shook his head as if suddenly aware he was babbling.

"No, thank you," Jake said.

Ross set his backpack on the floor. "None for me."

Both men had, Amanda thought, made wise choices. The coffee was probably store brand instant.

She gathered up the mugs from the table and carried them to the kitchen to refill. She couldn't drink any more of the tea, but Dawson needed something to do with his hands. He probably wouldn't notice if she just put water in his mug. It might taste better.

"You've worked on kidnappings before?" Dawson asked Ross.

"I finished a case a few weeks ago. We found the kidnappers and got the boy back alive. The bad guys are in jail and the boy's home with his family."

Amanda turned at the solemn sound of the man's voice and saw that he was no longer smiling and being charming. His expression had turned serious, his features determined, his own notebook and pen on the table in front of him.

She returned to the table and set another cup of hot tea in front of Dawson then took a seat at the table between him and Daggett.

Charley floated over and stood between Daggett and her. She crossed one leg over the other and deliberately swung her foot through his immaculate khakis.

"Why did you do that?" He made a futile attempt to look innocent. "I just want to be close so I can hear everything that's said."

"We did some checking at Grant's school—" Daggett began.

"What?" Eyes wild, Dawson leaned across the table toward him. "You talked to them? What if the kidnappers find out?"

"They won't." Ross spread his hands over the table top between Jake and Dawson. "We've done this before. We know how to do it. Trust me. We're going to bring your brother home safe."

That sounded as if they believed there really was a brother.

It sounded as if Dawson wasn't crazy. That was good.

But that meant Dawson's brother really had been kidnapped. That was bad.

"Amanda told me the basics of your story," Jake said, "but I'd appreciate it if you'd tell me everything, all about your parents' deaths, changing your identities, Grant's disappearance, everything. You never know what small detail will help us find him."

Dawson clutched his cup in both hands and repeated the story he'd told Amanda, unwavering in the specifics.

When he concluded, Jake nodded. "That agrees with the information we have. The disappearance of you and your brother right after the murder of your parents was an unsolved mystery until today."

Disappearance of you and your brother. The brother had not died in the car crash. At least Amanda knew for sure what they were dealing with now.

Dawson nodded. "My dad knew those people were evil. He was prepared."

56

"Yeah, he did a good job. Your story was big at first, your parents dead from a car bomb and the two of you missing. But with no clues, the case went cold pretty fast. Then about a month after the incident, your uncle showed up and made inquiries about the two of you."

Dawson's knuckles turned white as his grip on his cup tightened. "Uncle? I don't have an uncle. Mom was an only child, and Dad's brother died when he was a baby."

The air in the room became thick and still like the air before a summer storm.

"What was his name?" Ross asked, his question somehow ominous in the quiet of the room. "The brother who died."

"Lawrence. Lawrence Franklin Dawson. He was two months old. It was a crib death."

Ross and Jake exchanged quick, knowing glances.

"Was that the name the man used?" Amanda asked.

Even Charley seemed to be holding his breath, anticipating the answer.

Jake nodded. "Yeah. It was."

Again deep silence enveloped the room.

"That means," Amanda said, laying a hand on Dawson's arm and speaking softly, "either your dad lied to you about his brother's death or the man pretending to be your uncle was an imposter, someone who knew about your family."

Dawson's jaw clenched. "My dad never lied."

"He set you up to live a lie, provided you with false identities."

"He did it to protect us."

"From what?"

Dawson spread his arms. "From this! From Grant being taken. From people wanting to kill us."

"But they don't want to kill you," Jake said quietly. "They want the program your father wrote."

"And I don't have it."

"Can we see the e-mail you got from the kidnappers?"

Dawson nodded and handed them the e-mail he'd shown Amanda.

The two men studied the print-out.

"Educated," Jake said. "No bad grammar or misspellings."

Ross nodded. "Computer literate. Knows about source code and has the expertise to bounce the message all over the world so we can't track him."

"He could be saying *we* to make it sound like there's more than one person involved, but I'm going to guess there really is more than one. Kidnapping an eleven-year-old boy would be quite a task for one man."

"Could be one of them has a religious background since he put 666 in his e-mail name. Thinks it makes him appear threatening."

"Or that's what he wants us to believe. There's no religious context in the body of the message, so it could be something deliberately designed to mislead us."

As the two men pointed out things Amanda had not even considered, she felt completely useless, as if she'd wasted valuable time that morning doing inconsequential things like talking to the weird neighbors.

Well, she'd called in the cops, the experts. Now she could turn it all over to them. Let them do their job. Stay out of the way.

She glanced at Dawson. He leaned forward intently, listening to every word the two detectives said.

Finally they stood and Ross retrieved his backpack. "Can you show me your brother's room? I'd like to check it for trace evidence."

"You have something in there to check for trace evidence?" Dawson asked. "In that bag?"

Ross grinned. "Got my own little traveling laboratory in here. If your brother's kidnapper left so much as a skin cell, I'll find it."

"But it's not like on TV, is it?" Dawson asked, refusing to be comforted. "It's not as simple as just inputting the DNA sequence and letting the computer find a suspect, is it? Even if you find a suspect, that still won't tell you where my brother is."

Ross gripped Dawson's shoulder. "No, it won't be as easy as they make it seem on TV, but we can do it."

"While you're working on that, I'll go question the other tenants," Jake said.

"We already questioned two of them." Amanda sat up straighter. Maybe her earlier efforts hadn't been completely wasted after all. Maybe she had done something right.

Jake frowned. "You did? Who did you talk to? What did they say? I wish you hadn't done that before we got here."

So much for thinking she'd done something right. "Hey, we didn't contaminate them or anything. We just asked if they saw something suspicious, and they didn't."

"I'll talk to them again." He turned and started toward the door.

"No!" Dawson shot to his feet. "What if they're watching and see you talking to the neighbors after we already talked to them and figure out I called the police?"

Jake opened his mouth as if to protest, but Amanda laid a hand on his arm and looked at Dawson. "I'll go with him," she said reassuringly, "introduce him as my cousin. It'll be okay. You stay here and help Ross."

Dawson hesitated then sat back down. "Okay."

He trusted her, counted on her. That was a little scary.

"I think I'll come along too," Charley said. "Scout the places first and be sure nobody's waiting inside to blow you away."

Yeah, a ghost who could only make his presence known as a cold chill was going to be more effective than a cop with a handgun.

Amanda ignored him and turned to Jake. "Come on, cousin."

They had just stepped into the hallway, closing the door behind them, when Dawson's shout stopped them.

"Amanda! It's Grant!"

Jake yanked the door open and Amanda darted back in. "Where?"

Dawson pointed to his laptop. "Another e-mail just came in. Look."

The image showed a young boy, eyes wide with fear, sitting in a chair with a gun pressed to the side of his head.

Chapter Six

Jake yanked out a chair and sat down at the table again. Ross did the same and pulled the laptop close. Both men peered intently at the image on the screen.

"Look at the wall behind him. Rough wood. Could be a cabin, a shed, a barn. Not a finished room," Jake said.

"Gun's a Glock 17. That narrows it down to about a million. But look at the way he's holding it, palming the grip." Ross pointed to the anonymous fingers wrapped around the gun.

Amanda leaned over Jake's shoulder to get a closer look at the picture. The man's grip definitely looked awkward. His right hand was a little low, and he cupped his left hand under the bottom of the stock.

Jake nodded. "I see it. Probably not an experienced shooter. That point's in our favor."

Amanda studied the picture carefully, searching every detail. "What's Grant doing with his hands?"

"Clenching his fists," Jake said. "The boy's terrified but trying not to show it."

"Grant's not scared!" Dawson protested.

Amanda straightened and slid an arm around Dawson's tense shoulders. "Anybody with a gun pointed at his head would be scared. Been there, done that. Trust me, even Batman would lose his cool if somebody aimed a Glock at his bat mask."

Jake lifted his head and looked at Dawson. "She's right. If your brother wasn't terrified, I'd be worried they'd drugged him."

"Agreed," Ross said without looking up. "I don't even want to talk about what I did the first time somebody shoved a gun in my face. Look, I think that's a wooden ladder-back chair he's sitting in. They could be in an old farmhouse."

Jake returned his attention to the picture. "Possible."

"I'll go in for a closer look." Charley darted through the laptop, causing the image to ripple.

Amanda repressed the desire to say something rude. This was a critical situation and Charley just wanted to be the center of attention.

"Grant's driving!" Dawson exclaimed. "That's why he has his hands like that, as if they're clenching a steering wheel. He's trying to tell us that they drove him." He frowned and sagged into a chair. "That doesn't help, does it? Of course they drove him to wherever they are."

"Yeah, not like they could fly." Charley swooped around the room.

As soon as they were alone, Amanda would tell him what she thought of his flippant attitude when a child's life was at stake. He was getting farther and farther away from that white light.

Jake reached for the laptop and looked at Dawson. "Can you make it do that again?"

Dawson shook his head. "I didn't do it. Some sort of electrical fluke. Why do you want it to happen again?"

"I can do it," Charley boasted and darted through the computer several times.

Amanda clenched her teeth and resisted the urge to smack him. She wouldn't be able to hurt him and she'd look silly swatting at the air.

"You see it?" Jake asked.

Ross nodded. "Dawson's right. The movement does make it look like the kid's driving. The way he's holding his hands, he's trying to tell us something."

"Yes!" Dawson agreed excitedly, scooting his chair around to get a better look at the small screen. "He's not scared. He's lived through some terrible things. He's just a little kid, but he's brave. He's smart. He's trying to let us know where to find him."

Charley scowled. "Glad I could help. You don't need to thank me."

Amanda certainly had no intention of thanking him. He wasn't trying to help. He was only trying to get attention.

"Driving...a golf course?" Jake suggested.

"Maybe," Ross said. "There are plenty of them around. Probably have a lot of tool sheds with unfinished walls on them. But that would be too public. They didn't gag him, so they aren't worried somebody will hear him scream."

"Not golf," Dawson said. "Grant plays baseball, no interest in golf. He wouldn't think of *driving* being a golf clue. It's got to mean actual driving, like in a vehicle."

Jake drummed his fingers on the tabletop. "Drive, car, bus, drive-in theater..."

"Hands on the wheel, turn the wheel, Ferris wheel, Ferris wheel at Fair Park," Ross contributed.

Dawson sat abruptly upright. "Wagon Wheel Park! In Coppell. About fifteen miles northeast of here. It's his favorite place to play baseball."

"That's brilliant!" Amanda enthused. And she hoped it was accurate. Dawson's expression had done an about-face from despair to hope. She didn't want to see him disappointed again.

"I've heard of it," Jake said. "Do they have cabins? Outbuildings? Something with rough walls?"

"No cabins, but they have lots of buildings. They have a tennis center and a gym and places you can rent for parties." Dawson stood, his excitement rising to a fever pitch. "We need to check it out."

Jake and Ross exchanged a look that didn't bode well for Dawson's enthusiasm.

"We'll check it out, but it's a long shot that he's actually being held in the park. That would be too public, too many people around," Jake said quietly.

"It's not all crowded with people," Dawson insisted, refusing to let his enthusiasm be dampened, to lose the sudden thread of hope. "There's nature trails and lots of open land and trees in the park as well as on the way there. Acres of places he could be."

"Yeah," Jake agreed. "Acres. That's a lot of land to cover and still keep a low profile. We'd need to bring in our search and rescue team. The only way to cover that much ground would be with a lot of men, dogs and helicopters."

"No!" Dawson shook his head. "We're taking a chance on Grant's life by having the two of you here. You read what they said. They'll kill him if they know I've talked to you. I'll go look for him myself."

He took a step toward the door, but Amanda moved in front of him, blocking his way. "Your bike's at the shop." And he still wasn't in any shape to be riding it.

"I'll take the truck."

"I'll drive you in the truck."

Ross stood, lifting his backpack. "Actually, I need Dawson to stay here to answer questions while I go through Grant's room."

Jake rose too. "I'll drive out there and look around."

"I'll go with you." Amanda picked up her purse and started toward the door.

"No, you won't," Charley and Jake said at the same time.

Amanda looked at both of them in amazement. "Yes, I will. What makes either of you think you can stop me?"

"Either of us?" Jake looked around the room. "You or, uh, Ross."

Ross looked bewildered. "I didn't say you can't go with Daggett. Boy makes his own decisions."

For the first time, Amanda was thrilled to hear her cell phone ring and draw attention away from her blunder. Even if it was her mother, she'd answer it for a diversion. She yanked the phone from her purse and looked at the display. Sunny. "I forgot! Sunny and I are supposed to go for a bike ride then have dinner to celebrate my name change. I'll tell her I can't make it."

"Go," Dawson said, grabbing her arm and gazing intently into her eyes. "You need to go for a ride with Sunny."

He was trying to get rid of her? He thought she'd done so little to help that he wanted to send her away?

No. His expression was too anxious, his grip on her arm too tense.

"Take the scenic route and look around."

Of course! Jake Daggett might not allow her to come along on an official search, but she and Sunny could ride over to Wagon Wheel Park, take a few side trails, look around. Charley could look around too, cover more ground than they could, check into locked buildings, make himself useful for a change.

"Good idea," Jake said. "Go for a ride. Clear your head. It may help you think of something crucial about this case."

"Yeah, go," Charley encouraged. "Get away from these cops."

Amanda answered her phone.

"Where are you?" Sunny asked. "I'm here and your shop's closed. Is everything all right?"

"Not really, but I'll be there in five minutes." She disconnected the call, returned the phone to her purse and smiled. "Okay, I'm off for a fun ride. Later, guys."

Jake arched a suspicious eyebrow. "Where do you plan to ride?"

"Wherever we please."

His eyes narrowed and his gaze hardened. "I'm going to Wagon Wheel Park right now. I hope you're not planning to ride in that same direction by some wild coincidence."

"No, you're not going there, are you, Amanda?" Charley asked. "Tell him you're not planning to go anywhere near there. You don't need to go the same place he's going."

Amanda hoisted her purse onto her shoulder, looked Jake directly in the eye and tilted her head indignantly. "Did you really just try to tell me where I can or can't ride my motorcycle? I've been choosing my own routes for a lot of years. I don't think you'll find anything in the Constitution that gives you the right to dictate where I ride. That's balls, Daggett, really balls."

He sighed but had the balls not to look even a little bit intimidated. "Let me put it this way. Should you happen to find yourself in the vicinity of Wagon Wheel Park and see anything even slightly suspicious, do me a favor and don't go charging in with some crazy idea of saving the world. I've got a big caseload right now, and I'd just as soon not have to look for your killer too."

"If I get killed, I'll see that somebody else gets my case." Amanda whirled away from him, heading toward the door.

"Do you have my cell number?"

Amanda stopped. Having a cell number for a cop might be a good thing. Having a cell number for a really attractive though annoying cop was an even more enticing thought. She turned back. "No, I don't.

68

What is it?" She took out her phone and located the listing for his work number. He gave her his cell number and she tapped it in. "Got it. Thanks." She looked at him and found him looking at her. That was normal. They were talking to each other. Of course they'd be looking at each other. But there was something compelling about his expression, something personal.

"I'm going to be in the vicinity," he said, "so you might think about giving me a call instead of doing something stupid like you did in Silver Creek."

Or maybe she'd imagined that brief personal look in his eyes, seen what she wanted to see.

She thrust out her jaw. "What I did? Thanks to my actions, you got Roland Kimball handed to you on a platter." She opened the door and stomped down the stairs, her motorcycle boots making satisfying thuds.

−✾−

Amanda pulled into the parking lot of her shop and brought the ancient truck to a shuddering stop. One day they probably ought to do some work on it, but working on bikes was much more fun. And more profitable.

A few feet away in the shade of a big live oak, Sunny leaned against her black Harley Crossbones. She'd chosen the dark color in a futile attempt to maintain the image of a sedate lawyer in Silver Creek. Her black leather jacket lay draped over the handlebars and she clutched her helmet under one arm.

She waved as Amanda got out of the truck. Her long, curly red hair, so much like Amanda's except she had a few white strands, was pulled back into a braid, the same as Amanda's. The optimum style for motorcycle riding. But they had both chosen to wear their hair long. Amanda chose to view that as a mother-daughter connection.

She returned the wave as she strode toward Sunny, a smile tilting her lips in spite of her distress over Dawson's situation. Sunny had that effect on her, made her feel that, even if something was wrong, it could be fixed.

"Get your real name back?" Sunny asked.

"Sure did, and I'm never giving it up again."

Sunny smiled, and for just a moment she looked like a mother, a wise, caring mother who knew her daughter would encounter a lot of unknowns in the future that could jeopardize any utterance of the word *never*.

How different her life could have been if Sunny had raised her. She was pretty sure this woman would never have planned a baby shower with a cardboard cake and engraved invitations to be sent out to a group of people whose personalities matched the cake.

"Irene sent you some cookies." Sunny withdrew a plastic container from the bag on the back of her bike.

A beam of warm Texas sunshine wrapped around Amanda's heart as she accepted the container prepared by her mother-in-law. "Irene. She and

Herbert are the only good things that came out of my marriage to Charley."

"Hey!" he protested.

"I have the absolute best in-laws in the world."

"You do," Sunny agreed. "Take your cookies upstairs, get your gear, and let's hit the road."

"First we need to talk. We have to do more than a fun ride today. We have a mission. Dawson's little brother has been kidnapped."

Sunny frowned. "Dawson's little brother? I didn't know he had one."

"I didn't either. Come upstairs with me and I'll tell you all about it."

They walked up the steps and into Amanda's apartment over the bike repair shop while she recited the events of the morning.

"How awful for Dawson and his brother," Sunny said. "You did the right thing, calling in the police. They'll find him."

Amanda set the container of cookies on her lamp table. "You say that like you're reciting lines from a book. You don't really believe it, do you?"

Sunny bit her lip. "Most kidnappings are resolved successfully within the first twenty-four hours. But since this one involves people who've already committed murder and they're asking for such a strange ransom..." She shook her head. "I don't know. It's a scary situation."

That wasn't what Amanda wanted to hear, but she appreciated the fact that Sunny was honest with her, that she treated her as an equal. They had thirty-two years to make up for and total honesty, even when it might be painful, was a good start.

"Do you think we have a chance of finding something by riding around today?"

Sunny met her gaze. "We might. It's a long shot, but we won't know until we try."

More honesty. Damn.

Amanda nodded. "A long shot is better than no shot. Which reminds me, I need to get one more thing."

She went to her bedroom and took from her nightstand drawer the .38 she'd bought in Silver Creek from Charley's friend, Dub. She checked to be sure it was loaded then returned it to the holster.

"You're taking a gun?"

Amanda jumped and whirled around. She hadn't realized Sunny had followed her into the bedroom. "Better to have a gun and not need it than need a gun and not have it."

Sunny studied her for a long moment, concern flickering in her eyes, then she nodded. "Good point." She turned and left the room.

Amanda released a sigh. For a brief instant she'd feared there'd be a battle. Her mother had never approved of her learning to shoot or having a firearm around. If she'd been there, they'd have had a *discussion*. Of course, Sunny owned several guns and had, in fact, saved Amanda's life a couple of months ago.

Yeah, her life could have been very different.

She shoved the gun into her purse, retrieved a helmet, gloves, and jacket from the closet and headed back to the living room.

Sunny grinned as she entered with her gear and the gun in her purse. "We don't need a DNA test to prove you're my daughter."

It was a simple statement, but it made Amanda feel warm inside.

༲✥

Out on the highway going seventy miles an hour the rush of air dissipated the summer heat and Amanda was comfortable even in her leather jacket and helmet. They stayed on the interstates until they reached the outskirts of Dallas, then Amanda exited and slowed as they rode past businesses and along streets with open fields on both sides.

Charley suddenly darted in front of Amanda then back again, waving his arms. That was strange. Usually he chose to hover on the back of her bike, pretending he was riding.

But he had done that same thing one other time, the time in Silver Creek when somebody had been following her. She pulled over to the side of the road and stopped.

Sunny followed suit and lifted the shield on her helmet. "What's up? Bike trouble?"

"No. I..." Amanda looked at Charley. "I think somebody's following us."

"Yes," Charley confirmed. "There's a beige minivan that's been on your tail since you left your shop. I thought at first it was a coincidence, but when he followed you off the highway, I knew."

"Somebody's following us?" Sunny repeated. "How do you know that?"

Amanda flinched. She could tell Sunny that she'd seen something in her rear view mirror, but that would be a lie. She and Sunny didn't lie to each other. However, she couldn't very well say Charley had told her.

A beige minivan drove up behind them, pulled off the road and stopped.

Chapter Seven

Amanda yanked off her helmet and gloves, reached into her purse strapped to the sissy bar of her bike, and wrapped trembling fingers around the grip of her gun. She got off her bike, holding the gun behind her, and turned to face the van. Her heart pounded so loudly she felt sure Sunny would hear it and know what a coward she was.

The ominous minivan was probably completely innocent. They had only Charley's word that it had been following them. Though he had lost the ability to lie in his current state, he was often mistaken and had a tendency to be melodramatic.

"They're getting out!" Charley warned, hovering behind Amanda.

Sunny swung off her bike and strode toward the van. She was tall and slim and at that moment she looked ten feet tall. A mother defending her child. A burst of happiness shot through Amanda in spite of the situation as she hurried to catch up with Sunny. She was, after all, the one with the gun. She would defend Sunny.

Both van doors opened and a man and woman got out.

"Get back," Amanda said as she walked faster, trying to pass Sunny.

Sunny stepped in front of her. "You get back. I've got this one."

"You ladies need some help?" the man asked, stepping away from the door and closing it. He didn't look like a serial killer. Average height, a little overweight, bald. The woman coming out the passenger side door was small and mousy.

But if serial killers looked dangerous, nobody would ever get in the car with them. Amanda moved to stand beside Sunny so she could get a clear shot.

"I'll go check it out." Charley darted through the roof of the van.

"Thanks, but we're fine," Sunny assured the couple.

The man nodded. "Saw you stop and thought you might be having bike problems. I used to ride. I know how tough that can be, stranded miles from nowhere."

"No problems. Just stopped to take some pictures," Amanda said.

The man glanced around them at the flat landscape dotted with mesquite trees and scrub oak.

Even Sunny gave Amanda a questioning look.

"It's a stark kind of beauty." Amanda shifted her grip around the gun. Her fingers were starting to sweat.

"I do a little photography myself. Just a hobby. What kind of camera you using?" The man walked closer to them. Though his stomach was rounded, his legs beneath his shorts were thin and pale. Not an intimidating figure, but Amanda felt somehow intimidated.

Ridiculous, she told herself. She was overreacting to Charley's melodrama.

"Just the camera in my cell phone."

Sunny took a step closer to the man, and Amanda took two steps.

"Thanks for stopping to see if we need help," Sunny said. "We're fine and really need to get on with our ride. We want to get back to Dallas before dark."

Charley burst through the windshield of the van, his eyes wide. "It's them! It's the kidnappers! They have blankets they could have wrapped him in and rags that probably have chlorophyll on them!"

"Chlorophyll?" Amanda repeated.

"Chlorophyll?" Sunny sounded even more astonished than Amanda.

The man from the van halted a few feet away and looked puzzled at the odd turn the conversation had taken.

Charley settled beside Amanda and pointed to the van. "You know. That stuff they use to knock people out."

Chloroform. Amanda doubted that the frumpy couple had kidnapping tools in their van, but she made a mental note of the license plate anyway. Charley wasn't always wrong. Most of the time but not always.

Sunny turned to Amanda. "Ready to get on the road again? Think you have enough pictures?"

Amanda gave a final glance at the man and woman standing beside the van. The woman was watching them with a strange expression. An expression of guilt because she had blankets and chloroform in her van or just curiosity about why Amanda suddenly blurted out the word *chlorophyll*?

"I'm ready. I have enough pictures." She turned, moving her gun around to the front to keep it out of sight of the couple in the van, and followed Sunny across the dusty shoulder of the road to their bikes.

"What are you doing?" Charley waved his arms wildly as he floated beside her. "Don't let them get away!"

Sunny lifted her helmet but paused before putting it on and looked back toward the van. "That was a little strange."

The man and woman back inside the vehicle, consulting a map spread out on the dash.

"Yeah, very strange. I thought everybody had GPS. Maybe they're looking for something that isn't on GPS, some place that doesn't have an address." Or maybe they were pretending to look at a map so they had an excuse for not leaving until Amanda and Sunny did.

"I wasn't talking about their map. I was talking about the way you suddenly shouted *chlorophyll*."

"Oh, yeah, about that..." Amanda searched her mind for an explanation that didn't sound insane. "It's a form of Tourette Syndrome." She flinched as the words came out of her mouth. So much for total honesty. The lie she'd just told Sunny seemed to hang between them like a visible shadow.

"No, it's not."

"No. It's not. We'll talk about it later. Let's get moving before those creepy people back there get on the road again."

"They were trying to be nice."

"Okay, they were nice creepy people. He just happened to be a former bike rider and he just happened to be a photographer. If we'd said we raised rats for fun and profit, I wonder if he'd have said he did that too?" She settled her helmet onto her head. "We've got a lot of ground to cover before dark."

As they rode away, Amanda looked in her rearview mirror. The van was still sitting there.

She was becoming paranoid and it was Charley's fault, but she had no idea how to get rid of him. Even Google couldn't find instructions for divorcing a dead man.

అ∾ఆ

The afternoon sun was sinking low on the horizon when Amanda and Sunny pulled to the side of the dirt road and parked for what seemed like the hundredth time.

"What do you think?" Amanda asked, pointing to the tumbledown shed a couple of hundred feet from the road. After riding around the area for over two hours, up and down side roads, stopping to peer into the occasional barn or out building, she understood why Jake hadn't been wildly enthusiastic about finding Grant from the possible clue. The area to be covered was daunting.

Sunny considered the dilapidated building. "If anybody was in there, they'd have to be holding up the roof with both hands."

Amanda sighed. "We might as well head home. This has been a wasted day. We haven't accomplished a thing."

"Yes, we have accomplished something. We covered a lot of ground. We know where Grant isn't being held."

That was a pretty lame attempt at encouragement, but Amanda let it go and mentally gave Sunny an *A* for *attitude*.

"Hang on, I'll check out this one," Charley said. "You ladies just stay here and don't get your motorcycle boots dirty. It's hard to use the brake on the bike with cow dung on your boot."

"How would you know?" Amanda flinched as soon as the words came out of her mouth. She had to stop talking to Charley in front of other people. "I didn't mean to say that."

Sunny moved closer and tentatively wrapped an arm around Amanda's shoulders. "I understand. You're upset and exhausted. You're allowed to be a little curt under the circumstances."

Sunny thought she had been replying to her comment about knowing where Grant wasn't being held. She didn't think Amanda was nuts, just rude. Amanda could deal with being thought a little strange, but not with being discourteous to someone she loved. "No," she said. "That's not—"

"Move closer!" Charley called, hovering a few feet from the shed. "This is as far as I can go."

He was restrained by that invisible leash. She could understand why Charley had been kicked out of heaven, but it seemed unfair she should be attached to him.

She moved away from Sunny, stepped a few feet into the field, and Charley disappeared inside the building.

"Amanda, what are you doing?" Sunny's tone suggested she now thought Amanda was nuts as well as rude. "Why are you walking into those weeds?"

"All clear!" Charley floated out of the structure and across the field.

Amanda turned to Sunny. "Just, uh, checking to see what kind of flower that is." Ouch! Another lie.

"It's a dandelion."

"Yes, so it is. A dandelion." Amanda gave a brief, phony laugh.

Sunny moved closer, concern creasing her brow. "Are you all right? We've been doing a lot of riding in this heat. Maybe we should rest for a while and drink some water. We could be getting dehydrated."

If only Charley could be explained by something as simple as dehydration. "Yes, water would be good. Water's always a good idea. Especially in the summer when it's hot."

"Wait in the shade of that tree and I'll bring you something to drink."

"That sounds good, but I don't need to wait in the shade. I'm okay. Really."

Sunny lifted a hand to Amanda's cheek. "You're flushed and hot. I'll grab a couple of bottles and we'll

81

drink them in the shade before we head out. Go on. I'll be right behind you."

Sunny's concern touched Amanda. She didn't hover the way her mother did or make a big production of it, but she was obviously worried about Amanda's health.

Her daughter's health.

Not that she had any reason to worry since Amanda was suffering from exposure to Charley rather than from exposure to the heat. Feeling a little pleased and a lot guilty, she obediently walked over to the mottled shade.

Sunny went to her bike, opened her pack and took out two bottles. "These were frozen when we started. They should still be a little cool." She joined Amanda under the tree, opened both and handed one to her.

"Thank you." Amanda took a long drink of the tepid water, trying to swallow her feelings of guilt for accepting Sunny's concern and care under false pretenses. The water went down nicely, but the guilt stuck halfway. "I have to tell you something," she blurted.

Sunny regarded her curiously. "Okay. I'm listening."

"I haven't been completely honest with you about some things, like how I knew somebody was following us or why I walked into that field."

"Okay," Sunny repeated, waiting quietly for Amanda to continue.

Amanda moved her bottle of water from one hand to the other, took another drink, looked at

Charley hovering beside her and tried to think of what to say next.

I see dead people. Well, not all dead people. Just one dead person.

"What if I told you that Charley's…um…essence is still around?"

The concern on Sunny's face intensified. "His essence? What are you saying?"

"His spirit. His soul." She swallowed hard. There was no good way to say it. "His ghost."

Charley scowled. "Damn it, Amanda, you know it hurts when you call me that."

"Ghost?" Sunny repeated. "You mean his memory? You're haunted by his memory? I didn't think you liked him very much."

Amanda drew in a deep breath and prepared to dive in headfirst. "No, not his memory. I'd happily forget about him if that was it. It's definitely his ghost."

"I'm not a ghost! I'm me!" he protested.

"You're a ghost."

"No," Sunny said quietly, the concern in her eyes ramping up another level. "I'm not."

Amanda tried to smile. "Of course you're not. I was talking to him. To Charley. To his ghost. But he doesn't like being called a ghost."

"I see. Amanda, you've had a really stressful day, physically and emotionally. Let's finish our water and go find something to eat. Your blood sugar's probably getting low. Did you eat lunch?"

"I skipped lunch and I am hungry, but food isn't going to change anything. Charley's ghost is still going to be here."

"He's here? Right now?"

Amanda nodded. "Standing next to me."

Sunny's worried gaze flickered from one side of Amanda to the other. "I don't see anything."

Too late to back down now. "I know you don't. I'm the only one who can see him. The irony is that I'm the one person in the world who has the least desire to see him."

Charley clutched at his heart as if wounded. "Ouch!"

"Amanda, there's nobody here except the two of us." Sunny moved closer, her tone still calm but the words edged with concern.

"You're correct. There's nobody except us, but there is also Charley's ghost. You can't see him. You can't hear him. You can't touch him. The only way you know he's there is the sensation of cold when he touches you."

Charley shoved his hands in his pockets and looked dejected. "First I'm a ghost, now I'm frigid. Do the insults never stop? Just wait until you try to get to the light. They'll kick you back too."

"Wave your hand right here." Amanda dragged her fingers through Charley's chest, shivering at the chill.

Her expression anxious, Sunny reached for the space Amanda indicated.

Charley zipped away. "Bad enough *you* do things like that to me. I can't let just anybody reach inside my body."

"He moved." It sounded lame to Amanda even as she said it.

"Of course he did. Let me get you some more water. Dehydration can cause a lot of problems."

"Like hallucinations? You think I'm hallucinating?"

"Yes. Like hallucinations."

"I don't want any more water. I'm already going to have to stop to go to the bathroom before we get to Dallas."

Sunny laughed abruptly, the sound a tinkle of magic in the dusty, mundane countryside. "That sounds more like my daughter."

And Amanda wanted nothing more than to please her, to earn the right to be called her daughter. But she couldn't do that by being deceitful. "Maybe this will convince you. After he came back as a ghost, Charley told me things. He told me that he broke into your office and found the file cabinet where you had pictures of me and my original birth certificate. Then he came to Dallas to meet me and blackmail my dad."

"Blabbermouth," Charley said.

Sunny paled, licked her lips, opened her mouth as if to say something then closed it again.

"I would have no way of knowing that if Charley hadn't told me," Amanda said.

"I believe Charley told you, just not his ghost. He told you while you were married to him, before he died."

"If he'd told me that, I'd have known you were my mother when I first met you. He was already dead by that time, remember? I didn't know. Not until the night you told me. Anyway, if he'd told me about trying to blackmail Dad, I'd have killed him and saved Kimball the trouble." She shoved her helmet on her head, strode to her bike, got on and started it before Charley could protest her statement or she could see Sunny's reaction.

This confession business was tough.

But she'd made the right decision even if it was going to be difficult to convince Sunny of Charley's unreal reality. Deceit had no place in a close relationship. And, to her surprise, it was a relief to tell somebody else even if that somebody didn't believe her.

ঌ৽ঌ

When they got back to Dallas, they stopped for burgers and Amanda had to spend some time convincing Sunny she was rehydrated with stable blood sugar and could safely be left alone. She didn't mention Charley again and neither did Sunny, but the subject hung in the air between them, more palpable than Charley himself.

Outside the restaurant, Sunny gave her a quick hug. "I've got my cell phone in my pocket set on vibrate. Call me if you need me. Now. Later. In the middle of the night."

Sunny was worried. Needlessly.

But Amanda couldn't very well refuse the offer. She nodded.

"Promise?"

"I promise."

It was almost dark by the time Amanda got to Dawson's apartment.

"You look like you haven't slept in a week," she said when he answered the door.

"Yeah? Well, I feel like I haven't slept in two weeks." He moved aside for her to enter.

Jake sat at the table where the three laptops were up and running. Ross stood just outside Grant's room, zipping up his backpack.

"See anything today while riding nowhere near Wagon Wheel Park?" Jake asked.

Amanda set her helmet on the sofa and pulled off her jacket. She wanted to be able to tell him they'd learned something, wanted to throw in his face proof that her search had not been completely futile.

"Tell him about the van," Charley urged.

Oh, yeah, she could report the totally boring story of how she and Sunny had pulled off the road and a van with two ordinary people stopped to offer them help.

"No," she said. "I didn't see anything of interest on my ride. How about you?"

Jake's lips thinned as if in frustration and he shook his head. "I drove around the area. It's a big area. Even if we brought in a search team, it would be tough."

"And they'd kill Grant if they saw people searching," Dawson said.

"Heard anything else from *them*?" she asked.

"No." Dawson sat at the table in front of two of the laptops. "I've been going through everything on all our computers again." He no longer sounded panicked. Now he sounded dull, detached, dead inside. "Maybe I could give them all three of these computers and they can find what they want."

Amanda refrained from saying that did not sound like a very good plan. She looked at Jake and then Ross. Neither one of them appeared any more hopeful than she felt.

"We may have some leads," Ross said. "I need to get everything I collected back to the lab."

"What did you find?" Amanda asked, suddenly hopeful. "Fingerprints? DNA? Fibers?"

Ross laughed at her eagerness and hefted the bag onto his back. "Maybe. Among other things, I found some blue fibers that could be from a blanket, and Dawson said he's never had a blue blanket."

"That blanket in the van was blue!" Charley darted over to stand beside Ross. "Tell him about the beige minivan."

"A blue blanket?" Amanda repeated. "There are probably thousands of blue blankets around."

"Yeah," Ross agreed. "But every small piece of information we find narrows the scope and gets us closer to the truth. Add the blue blanket to the beige minivan..." He shrugged.

Amanda's breath caught in her chest. "Beige minivan? What beige minivan?"

Ross nodded toward Jake. "My buddy had a little luck too."

Amanda looked at Jake. He scowled and shook his head slightly.

"Tell me!" she demanded. "We've got to work together on this. You can't pull that *official police business* on me. I'm involved too."

"The lady downstairs," Dawson said. "Detective Daggett talked to the people on the first floor and he found somebody who saw a beige minivan leaving early this morning."

She whirled on Jake. "Really? You can tell Dawson but not me? I'm the one who called you in on this!"

"Dawson doesn't use the information to go out and do crazy things."

"I'm going to do something crazy if you don't tell me everything. Dawson will tell me anyway if you don't."

Jake lifted his hands defensively. "Okay, okay. I talked to an exotic dancer who got home around 3:00 a.m. She said she saw a beige minivan. She only noticed it because it was pulling away from in front of the building at three in the morning. Not many people out and about at that hour. But she didn't get a license plate, and there are an awful lot of beige minivans in Dallas."

Charley dropped his head into his hands. "I don't remember the license plate number."

"I do."

Chapter Eight

"You do what?" Jake asked.

Damn! She really needed to get better at not talking to Charley in public. "I do have a license number for a beige minivan. This may be a coincidence, but Sunny and I saw one today." She described the encounter, omitting the part about Charley seeing a blue blanket though without that bit of information, the story seemed inconsequential, a coincidence.

Jake and Ross exchanged glances. Ross set his backpack on the floor. "What color hair did the woman have?"

"Kind of a light brown, mousy blond. Why?"

"Short or long?"

"Short, and the man was bald. Why are we talking about hair?" She thought of his answer when she asked if he'd found DNA. *Among other things...*

Ross shook his head. "I found a couple of long blond hairs in Grant's room."

"Oh. No, it didn't belong to either one of those people. Her hair was very short and his was nonexistent."

"Tell him about the blue blanket," Charley insisted.

Other than claiming she had x-ray vision, Amanda couldn't think of a single way to bring that blue blanket into the conversation. Besides, a blue blanket in a beige minivan was not exactly a unique occurrence.

"The van's worth checking into," Jake said. He took his notepad from his pocket and wrote down the number as Amanda recited it.

Jake and Ross left, and Amanda sat down at the table with Dawson. She was exhausted and wanted desperately to get home to her bed, but she hated to leave Dawson alone. Not likely he'd get any sleep that night.

He typed rapidly on one of the laptops.

"Have you found something?" she asked.

"Yes." He moved the mouse, clicked and looked at her, his gaze feverish. "I found the license plate."

"What?" That was not the answer she'd expected, though she probably should have. Dawson would have started hacking away as soon as she verbalized the number. Daggett and Ross would have to go through regular channels to find it. Dawson suffered from no such constraints.

He shot up from his chair. "One of the women next door, the ones who weren't home this morning. It's her license plate! And she has long blond hair!" He charged toward the door.

Amanda lunged after him. "Wait. I've got Jake's cell number. They're probably still downstairs on the way to their car. We can catch them."

Dawson wasn't listening. He was already out the door.

She yanked her cell phone out of her purse and tried to hit the button to call Jake as she hurried after Dawson.

By the time she reached the hall, he was already banging on the door of apartment 3A.

Jake answered his phone.

"Get back up here now," she said and disconnected. No time to explain.

An attractive brunette opened the door of 3A and smiled. "Hi, Dawson."

"Does your blond roommate have a beige—how do you know my name?"

Her smile widened. "You live next door to me. I've talked to your little brother. He's not as shy as you are."

"You talked to Grant?"

She held the door wider. "Come on in. I'm Megan Thornton, and this is my roommate, Hannah Wilder." She indicated a blond woman sitting on the sofa with a book in her lap.

Grant's kidnapper?

"Don't go in there!" Charley warned.

"Grant's missing," Dawson blurted.

"He's missing?" Megan's hand shot to her mouth. "What do you mean?"

Once again somebody needed to take charge, and it wasn't going to be Charley or Dawson. Amanda shoved her assistant into the apartment and followed him in. "Hi. I'm Dawson's friend, Amanda Caulfield."

Megan looked a little disappointed at those words. She had seemed happy enough to see

Dawson. Was it possible there could be some romantic interest there? Probably not if she was involved in Grant's kidnapping. But that wasn't proven yet.

"His employer friend," Amanda amended just in case. "We need to talk to you about Hannah's beige van." Not her choice of how to start a conversation, but they didn't have time to dink around.

Hannah rose from the sofa. "I don't have a van. I drive a red Kia."

Dawson looked from one girl to the other and blinked a couple of times. "What's your license plate number?"

Hannah and Megan looked at each other and frowned. "What's this about?" Megan asked.

"As Dawson said, his brother is missing, and a beige van with your license plate number is, uh, a vehicle of interest." Amanda recited the digits. "Is that your number?"

Hannah looked confused. "Maybe. I don't know. Who remembers their license plate number?"

"I do," Dawson replied.

"Of course you do," Amanda said. "You probably remember the address of the hospital where you were born. Hannah, would you be willing to take us downstairs to the parking lot to check the license plates on your car? It's important."

"Sure, if it'll help find Grant." She retrieved a ring of keys from her purse.

"I'll go too." Megan opened the front door.

"I'm so sorry," Hannah said. "Grant's a great little guy. Last week he helped me carry my groceries upstairs. The bag wasn't heavy, but he wanted to help."

Halfway down the second flight of stairs they met Jake and Ross coming up.

"What's wrong?" Jake asked.

Amanda paused while the others continued downstairs. "We have to go to the parking lot to check Hannah's car. Dawson traced the plates to her but she says she drives a red Kia."

"How did he trace—?"

"Don't ask. Let's just go check it out." She pushed past him, following Dawson and the girls to the parking lot in back.

"That's my car." Hannah pointed. Even in the darkness, the vehicle was obviously small and red.

Amanda looked around at the dozen or so vehicles in the lot. Not a beige minivan to be seen. She felt a stab of disappointment. They were back to ground zero. No leads. No clue how to find a little boy who must be very scared by now. She thought of the raggedy dog in Grant's bed. He would be sleeping without it tonight.

"That's not the license plate." Dawson moved closer to the car. "Maybe I got the numbers wrong."

Amanda shook her head. "We know that's not possible. Maybe *I* got the numbers wrong."

"That's possible," Jake said.

He was only agreeing, but Amanda thought it rather rude of him to do it so readily. "Or maybe I didn't." Her hopes rose. "Maybe—maybe somebody switched the license plates. Don't you think it's a pretty big coincidence that those plates led Dawson to his next-door neighbor?"

"She's got a point," Ross said.

Jake took his notebook from his pocket and wrote down the number of Hannah's plates. "Why don't we go back upstairs and Dawson can do whatever illegal search he just did to find out where this license plate leads us?"

Taking two steps at a time, Dawson led the group back upstairs and was already inside his apartment when Amanda reached the third floor.

She was halfway across the landing with the others close behind when the door of 3B opened and Nick Farner stepped out. "I thought I heard you coming up the stairs. You have a distinctive step. Did you find the missing boy?"

"No, we're still looking," Amanda said.

"Hi, Nick." Megan waved then hurried on into Dawson's apartment.

Jake and Ross paused, their attention riveted on the newest addition to the melee.

Hannah stopped beside Ross. "Hi, Nick. They're looking for a beige van. You know anybody with a beige van?"

He shook his head. "No beige vans. I drive a beige Honda. Finally decide to call in the cops?" He inclined his head toward Jake and Ross.

"No!" Amanda grabbed Jake's arm to prevent him from saying anything. "No, this is my cousin Jake and his partner Ross." Jake and Ross both whirled to look at her in amazement. Hannah's eyes widened and she moved a step away from Ross.

95

Amanda flinched as she realized she'd just identified Ross as Jake's partner, pretty much told Nick they were cops. "I mean, his friend. This is Jake's friend Ross."

Charley burst into laughter. "Way to go, Amanda!"

Nick grinned and winked. "Nice to meet you, Jake and Ross. I'm good with *partners*."

Amanda looked from Jake to Ross as the dual meaning of her words hit her. "I mean, they're friends. They don't live together or...or...anything." Amanda felt her face flush and wished she could sink through the floor, all the way down to the ground and then a few feet under.

"Keep talking, Amanda!" Charley laughed harder. "You're making it better with every word out of your mouth!"

"I..." Amanda began with no idea of what she was going to say.

"I found it!" Dawson called.

"Bye, Nick. Gotta run." Amanda, happy to take advantage of the diversion, took Jake's arm and turned him toward Dawson's apartment.

He shot her a bemused glance but followed her inside.

Dawson looked at Hannah. "The license plate currently on your car is not registered to you or your car."

"What? I don't understand." Hannah tried to peer over his shoulder, but Dawson closed his laptop. Probably didn't want Jake or Ross to see what database he'd illegally hacked into.

"The license plate currently on your car traces to a silver Ford Escort that was retagged in Kansas City a year ago when the owner died and the car was sold."

Even Charley was silent for a few moments, digesting the implications of this latest piece of the puzzle.

Jake looked around the room. "We'd better let these ladies get back home. Sorry for the misunderstanding about your car."

"We don't mind helping," Megan protested. "We like Grant and we've been wanting to get to know Dawson."

"We'll start again tomorrow after everybody has a good night's sleep," Ross said.

"Before you go," Amanda said, stepping between Megan and the door, "I have a question. You both seemed to know that guy we were just talking to, Nick."

"Sure," Hannah said. "He moved into his grandmother's place a couple of weeks ago."

"His grandmother's place?" That explained the grandmotherly furnishings. "What happened to his grandmother?"

"He killed her," Charley said. "I told you he's a nut job. I knew Mr. Muscles wouldn't buy that kind of furniture on purpose."

"She's taking a cruise to Alaska with her bridge club," Hannah said.

Jake moved up behind Amanda. "Did you know the grandmother?"

"Sure. Mrs. Lowell's a nice lady. We sometimes take her trash downstairs for her since she has trouble with the steps, and she makes cookies for us."

"She has trouble with the steps?" Ross asked.

"She has a bad knee."

"Would she go on a trip with a bad knee? Did she tell you she was going?"

"No. Nick said it happened really fast, that she got the chance to go and he was moving to town, so it all worked out well for everybody."

"Did you meet Nick before he moved in? Did he come to visit his grandmother often?" Jake asked.

Megan frowned. "Why are you asking all these questions about Nick?"

"Do you think he had something to do with Grant's disappearance?" Hannah asked.

"No, of course not," Ross reassured her.

Good grief. The girls weren't dumb. "Maybe," Amanda said. "He's new in the building, so it's something we need to consider."

"Wow," Hannah said.

"Freaky," Megan added.

"Did Mrs. Lowell ever talk about her grandson? Show you pictures?"

Hannah glanced around the room and folded her arms as if cold or nervous. "She never mentioned him and we never saw him visit. Of course, we're gone a lot. We both go to grad school and work."

Megan swallowed and moved closer to Hannah. "One day he was there and she wasn't. You think he's not really her grandson?"

"If she never mentioned him, that doesn't sound like a proud grandmother," Amanda said.

"But if he's not her grandson, what's he doing in her apartment?" Hannah asked. "Is she okay?"

"Of course she is." Jake scowled at Amanda.

"We'll find out tomorrow," Ross promised.

"Okay." Megan looked toward the door.

Amanda opened it and both girls started through.

Hannah turned back to Ross and smiled. "You're really cute. If you ever change your mind about—" she tilted her head in Jake's direction— "your partner, give me a call."

Amanda shut the door behind the girls.

Ross' gaze lingered on the closed door for a moment before he turned to Amanda. "After we find Grant I think I'm going to kill you."

Jake nodded. "I'll help."

Charley didn't need to worry about anything going on between Jake and her. Amanda had taken care of that all by herself.

Chapter Nine

Jake moved across the room and sat down at the table with his ubiquitous pen and notebook. "Let's sum up what we've got so far."

Dawson brought up a blank Word document on his laptop.

Ross and Amanda settled in the remaining seats.

Charley sat cross legged in the middle of the table, his expression pleased and happy. "Detective Daggett's ticked off at you."

Amanda looked away from Charley and focused on the screen of Dawson's laptop. "Write this down. Stolen license plate with a Kansas City connection."

"The plates were not necessarily stolen," Jake said. "The new owner may have just thrown them away when he got the car retagged in Kansas City. But why the double switch? Why change plates with Hannah's car rather than just use the discarded Missouri plates? Did they not realize it would be easy for us to track both plates?"

"They weren't expecting us to be called in," Ross said. "But they know Dawson is technically savvy. They went to a lot of trouble to get phony plates and then add another layer to the deception by switching the plates. My take on the license plate thing, they're buying time, diverting attention away from themselves, making it as difficult as possible for us...anybody...to track them so they'll have time to get away. They're detail-oriented and clever, but the trouble they went to in order to confuse us is overkill. They're trying too hard. I don't think they're professionals."

Dawson stopped typing. "So you're saying amateurs have my brother? What does that mean?"

"Amateur criminals," Jake said. "That's good for us. They're trying really hard to cover all the bases, but if they haven't done this before, they may miss something, something we can use to find them."

Ross nodded. "They're counting on you not getting professional help, Dawson. But you did, and that gives us an edge."

Amanda thought it sounded like the boys were feeding Dawson a load of malarkey to make him feel better, but that was not necessarily a bad thing. Dawson had aged ten years in the past twelve hours. He needed some hope. "Maybe those people in the van were following Sunny and me because they thought I was going to get professional help."

"That's a possibility," Jake said. "Are you sure they were following you, that they didn't just happen to be going in the same direction?"

"I'm sure," Charley said. "I saw them following you all the way from your shop."

"I'm pretty sure. I saw them in my rearview mirror several times all the way from the shop." Lying to Jake was much easier than lying to Sunny. He kind of invited it, suggesting she didn't know the difference between a van going in the same direction and a van that was following her. Of course, it had been Charley who'd noticed, not her. But that was immaterial.

"I see." Jake drummed his fingers on the tabletop. "If they weren't following you but were just going toward Wagon Wheel Park, that could mean we were right about the area where Grant's being held. If they *were* following you..." He shrugged. "Then all we know is that they were following you. We have no idea why. Are you absolutely certain you saw them behind you when you left your shop?"

Amanda looked at Charley. She had only his word that the people were following her, and if he was wrong, they could miss a lead on the case.

Charley spread his arms, hands out. "I'm certain, okay? I know what you're thinking, but I can't lie now, remember? Whatever I say, you can take it as gospel."

Amanda looked up toward the ceiling, half expecting a crash of thunder and lightning as the word *gospel* came out of Charley's mouth. When it didn't happen, she straightened and looked Daggett in the eye. "I'm sure. Either they were following me, or they just happened to be in the vicinity of my motorcycle shop when Sunny and I rode out and going in the same direction all the way out of town."

"Maybe they followed you because they saw you were heading in the direction of where they were holding Grant," Dawson suggested. "Maybe they wanted to find out how much you know."

"That's also a possibility," Jake said.

"I'm not convinced that Hannah isn't involved," Dawson said. "She's got long blond hair, and the

102

license plate on the van belongs to her. I'll see what else I can find out about her."

"I'll check her out tomorrow," Ross said, "but I don't think she's a part of this."

Jake laughed. "Yeah, of course you believe a beautiful woman who thinks you're cute is innocent. But you're only going to be able to check her out on the computer. No point in trying to check her out personally after what our friend here told her about us."

"I wasn't thinking!" Amanda lifted her hands in the same defensive posture Charley had used earlier. "I just meant that you two are partners, like cop partners. But as soon as I said it, I realized I shouldn't be implying you're cops so I tried to fix it and that's when I said—"

"Keep talking, Amanda." Charley regarded her with a smiling, satisfied expression. "I don't have to worry about Detective Daggett hitting on you now. He'll never speak to you again and neither will this other guy."

Dawson looked up from his laptop. "You told Hannah that Jake and Ross were partners?" For the first time during the course of that long day, a smile tilted the corners of his mouth.

"Exactly!" Amanda exclaimed, relieved at Dawson's attitude. "It's funny. One day you'll all tell this story and laugh about it. We could fast forward through time and start laughing about it now."

The corners of Jake's mouth tilted upward every so slightly. He ducked his head and returned his attention to his notebook. "Moving on to Nick. We need to get a last name for him."

"Farner," Amanda said.

"Good. And a first name for his grandmother. Then we need to check out his story."

Dawson's expression again became grim. "Check out Hannah, check out Nick. That takes time. We may not have time."

Jake laid a hand on his arm. "The clock isn't ticking yet. The kidnappers haven't given us a deadline. Ross and I are going to go home and get a little sleep, then we'll get back on this early tomorrow. Both of you need to get some sleep too."

"He's right," Amanda said. "I'm so tired I can't think straight."

Jake arched an eyebrow. "You hit that stage a few minutes ago when you introduced us to Nick."

Great. She had a smart-mouthed ghost and a smart-mouthed detective to deal with.

☜☞

"Amanda! Wake up! Do you hear me? Get up!"

Charley. Of course it was Charley. Who else would be demanding that she wake from her pleasant dream?

"Go away," she grumbled, then came suddenly wide awake as Charley's words brought back memories of crashing her motorcycle and Charley trying to wake her. Déjà vu.

But she wasn't lying on the ground in her motorcycle gear. She was lying on her bed having a wonderful dream of riding her motorcycle and hearing wind chimes. Not possible, of course, since the helmet and the engine noise would block out any such sound, but it had been a pleasant dream.

"I won't go away. I couldn't even if I wanted to. Get up. Dawson's calling you."

That explained the wind chimes. Her cell phone ring tone. Amanda shot up from the bed and grabbed the phone. "Dawson?"

"I fell asleep and just now checked my e-mail. It's them. They sent instructions. I have to get the program to them before six o'clock today. That gives us only fourteen hours to find it!"

Amanda looked at the clock. Four a.m. Still dark outside. She suppressed a yawn. "I'll be right there." With a six-pack of Coke and some decent tea.

She turned a sleepy gaze on Charley. "Do not follow me into the shower."

He widened his eyes in feigned innocence. "Of course not."

She didn't believe him but there was nothing she could do about it. She couldn't shower with her clothes on.

Half an hour later she arrived at Dawson's apartment and pounded up the stairs in her biker boots. As she sprang onto the third floor landing, Brendan Matthews, clad in a shiny silver helmet and matching jacket, burst from his apartment clutching a large, strange gun with coiled wires dangling from it.

Amanda stopped in her tracks, sucking in her breath, her hand going automatically to her purse. Damn! She'd left the apartment in such a rush, she'd forgotten her gun. "Brendan! I'm Dawson's friend, Amanda! Don't shoot!"

Brendan lowered the gun and straightened his glasses. "Amanda? Oh, yeah. I remember. They took Dawson's brother. I heard you and thought they were coming back."

Was he talking about the aliens again? Or maybe he'd actually heard the people when they came to take Grant although yesterday he'd said he'd never even seen the boy. "Did they make a noise like I did just now when I came up the stairs?"

Brendan frowned and rubbed the side of his nose. "Yes," he finally said. "They did sound like that except their armor rattled and clanked."

"Did you come out and see them like you came out and saw me just now?"

Brendan edged back into his apartment, his eyes wide behind his glasses. "Oh, no. I didn't see them. I didn't see anybody."

Amanda darted forward and wedged her foot in the door before he could close it. "You saw them, didn't you? You saw the people who took Grant."

"No!" Brendan lifted the gun again, and Amanda removed her foot from the door.

"Please! You need to tell us what you saw."

But the door closed firmly in her face.

"He knows something," Charley said.

Amanda nodded. "But I'm not sure we can pull it out of his tangled brain. I need to tell Jake and Ross." She took her cell phone from her purse.

"Why would you tell them? They were rude to you. Just tell Dawson."

Amanda looked at the door of 3D. "I don't think so. If I tell Dawson, he'll go nuts. Remember how he acted with Nick and then again with Hannah when he thought they were involved?" She shook her head. "We need professional help."

"It's too early. Your cop will still be sleeping. You don't want to wake him up."

"Sure I do. Why should Detective Daggett get any more sleep than I got?" She punched in the number on her cell phone.

Chapter Ten

Dawson—eyes bloodshot and a day's growth of beard stubbling his cheeks—answered Amanda's knock. He had a can of Red Bull in one hand and, judging by the way he twitched, it was not his first.

"How many of those have you had?"

He stepped back to allow her to enter his apartment. "Three. I went down to the all night convenience store on the corner and got some. I never had one before, but today I need to wake up and be alert so I can find the code they want." He closed and locked the door behind her.

"I don't suppose you've had anything to eat," she said.

"I'm not hungry." He was talking fast, nothing like his usual precise, unhurried speech.

"I am. I just talked to Daggett, and he's on his way over with food. You need calories to get your brain cells working. I brought Cokes and some Harney and Sons Hot Cinnamon Spice Tea. You may not need any since you have your caffeine-on-steroids drink, but I do."

"Detective Daggett's coming back? He can't help now. We're on deadline. We failed to find Grant. Now we just need to find the code so I can give it to them."

108

Amanda popped open a Coke, stored the rest in the refrigerator, set the box of tea on the counter and went to the table where Dawson still had three laptops going. "Show me the e-mail."

He turned one of the screens toward her.

From: johndoe666@e-mail.com

To: computerguy@e-mail.com

Copy the code to a thumb drive and deliver that thumb drive to locker 232 at the Fitness 4 You Club on Preston Road before 6:00 p.m. today. After we have verified the code, your brother will be returned to you unharmed. If you fail to do so or if you give us the incorrect code, we will excise one of your brother's fingers for every hour you delay. At midnight we will slit his throat and throw his body into a dumpster.

Do not attempt to attach a tracking device. Do not attempt to give us bogus code the way your father did. Anything of this nature will result in the removal of more fingers, all of which we will deliver to you.

Amanda frowned at the stilted language. "*Excise* his fingers? Who says *excise*? It sounds more like we're dealing with a college professor than a dangerous kidnapper."

"They're dangerous. They killed my parents."

A horrible thought occurred to Amanda. "Why did they kill your parents and ruin a chance to get this program? Wouldn't they want to keep them alive until they got what they wanted?"

"That's a good point," Charley agreed. "Sounds like they thought he gave them the program they wanted, but he gave them the wrong the code. Bogus code. So maybe they got mad and killed him for jacking them around." He shook his head. "No, that would be really dumb if they did that. If Dawson and Grant had been with them, everybody would be dead and they'd never get the right code."

The kidnappers were not dumb.

Dawson looked at her for a long moment, and she wished she hadn't asked the question. If Dawson's father gave them a bogus program but they didn't realize it at first and thought they had the right program, that meant they'd killed his parents as soon as they got what they wanted. And that probably meant they'd kill Dawson and Grant as soon as they got what they wanted from them.

"I don't know." Dawson straightened his glasses and took another drink of Red Bull.

Amanda sipped her Coke and said nothing. Dawson was smart. If he didn't see all the ramifications of her question, it was because he didn't want to and she was not going to point it out to him. He didn't need to add the possibility of murder-no-matter-what to his concerns, but she would add it to her list of things to tell Daggett.

Maybe if that list was long enough, he and Ross would focus on the important stuff and forget about what she'd said to Nick yesterday.

Daggett arrived half an hour later with six breakfast sandwiches. He looked the same as the day before. Faded jeans, cowboy boots and T-shirt stuffed with bulging biceps, pecs and deltoids.

"No donuts?" Amanda asked, pulling the warm sandwiches from the bag. "I thought cops loved donuts."

"I like those donuts with the little sprinkles," Charley said. "Not that your detective friend cares what I like."

"I'm not a cop, remember?" Jake grinned. "I'm your gay cousin."

Amanda flinched. He wasn't going to forget about yesterday.

She handed a paper-wrapped sandwich to Dawson. "You need to eat this."

He shook his head. "No, thanks. I'm not hungry." He lifted his Red Bull can to his mouth.

"I don't recall asking if you were hungry. I said, you need to eat this." Amanda tried to assume a bossy, dictatorial voice and speak as if she expected to be obeyed.

To her surprise, it worked. Dawson pulled back the wrapper and began to eat with one hand while working the keyboard with the other.

Apparently she was onto something with the bossy attitude. She and Daggett exchanged a glance and a shrug.

Jake took a bite of his own sandwich. "Show me the new e-mail."

Dawson indicated the laptop sitting beside the one he was using. "It's on there. Untraceable, just like the first one."

Jake pulled the computer toward him, scanned the message and frowned.

Amanda gulped down her greasy egg and sausage sandwich, surprised at how good it tasted. She had grabbed a couple of Irene's chocolate chip cookies on her way out the door that morning, but nothing substantial. "Dawson, while you eat and look for that code, Detective Jake and I are going outside to see if we can find, uh, shoe prints."

Jake swallowed the last bite of his sandwich and looked at her as if she'd lost her mind. "Shoe prints?"

Dawson, absorbed in his work, didn't notice the ridiculous statement she'd just made. "Okay."

"Yes. Let's go look *outside*." She twitched her head toward the door and winked.

That effort earned her another *are you nuts?* look.

She walked to the door, unlocked it and went into the hallway then turned back to see Jake still sitting at the table watching her curiously. She scowled and motioned for him to get out there with her. Jerk. He was being deliberately obtuse.

Finally he stood and followed her into the hall.

She closed the door firmly behind them.

"Shoe prints?" he asked as they walked downstairs. "We checked for footprints yesterday and found nothing in all this concrete. What was really in that Coke can?"

"It was just an excuse to get you out of Dawson's hearing." They reached the bottom floor and she pushed open the door to the outside world, to the cool, fresh air of the predawn summer day. She left the sidewalk and crossed the patchy grass, brown from summer heat and no rain, to the shadows of a

112

big catalpa tree, then turned to face him and bumped into his wide, solid chest. "Oh!" She lifted her hands automatically to brace herself. Okay, maybe it wasn't a completely automatic reaction. Maybe she'd kind of been looking for an excuse to touch that chest.

He grabbed her arms to steady her. "You okay?"

"Amanda! Stop pawing him!" Charley shouted in her ear.

She jerked away. "You were following too close."

Jake spread his hands and stepped back.

Damn. Between Charley and her ability to say stupid things, she probably wasn't going to have a lot of chances to touch Jake's chest or any other part of his anatomy. "I have some things I need to tell you that I don't want Dawson to hear."

Jake folded his arms. "I have some things to tell both you and Dawson. I stayed up late last night doing some checking, then somebody woke me up after only a couple of hours of sleep. But you go right ahead and tell me your news first."

Jake had news? That sounded promising. "My news is just a possibility. I don't know anything for certain. Tell me what you learned first."

"I'll tell you and Dawson at the same time so I don't have to repeat myself."

Annoying man. "Fine, then I'll be quick. The guy in 3C, the one who sees aliens, I think he saw the aliens who took Grant. I mean, obviously they weren't really aliens. But I think he saw them even though he said he didn't."

That got Jake's attention. He took her arms and leaned toward her. If Charley wasn't there...

But he was. He was always right there with her.

"Why do you think that?" Jake asked.

She told him about her encounter with tinfoil boy. "I didn't want Dawson to hear because I was afraid he'd freak out like he did when he thought Hannah was involved. You know, run over there and bang on the guy's door, try to beat him up. If Megan hadn't answered her door really fast last night, I think he would have broken it down. And he actually attacked Nick yesterday when he thought he heard a scream coming from the apartment."

Jake frowned and stepped back, turning loose of her arms. Darn. "Thought he heard a scream coming from the apartment? And you're just now telling me?"

"His cat was freaked out because—never mind. Not important. What's important is talking to Brendan about his aliens."

Jake nodded. "Okay. I'll go talk to him."

"He doesn't trust cops any more than he trusts aliens, so you'll have to go in as my gay cousin." She couldn't stop the smile that spread across her lips at her dig.

Jake refused to rise to the bait. "I'll do whatever needs to be done. If all else fails, maybe I could shove a few splinters under his fingernails to make him talk."

"I don't think that will be necessary." He was kidding. She was sure he was kidding. Pretty sure.

"You said you had two things. What's the other one?"

She repeated her theory that Dawson and Grant could be in danger even if he located and turned over to them the program they wanted.

"I know."

That sent a cold chill down her spine. "You know?"

"In my other life, I'm a cop. I know a few things about criminals. They tried to clean up all loose ends before. They'll do it again. After somebody kills once, every time after that it gets easier."

"Do you think Sunny and I are in danger? They were following us." If she'd put Sunny in danger, she'd never forgive herself.

"I think you'll be fine if you can back off and let Ross and me handle this. We're actually trained to do this sort of thing." He shoved his hands in his pockets. "But of course you can't back off. So, yeah, I think you're in danger."

The only response Amanda could come up with was, *You can really be a jerk when you try*, so she ignored his comment. "Let's go talk to tinfoil boy."

He followed her inside and up the steps to the third floor.

"Go hold Dawson's hand while I talk to 3C," he said.

Amanda gaped at him and reconsidered her decision to refrain from telling him he was a jerk. "No. Did you not listen to me? You need me to go with you as your cousin. I've met him and talked to him. We've bonded."

"Bonded? Really? He threatened you with a gun and closed the door in your face. That doesn't sound like any kind of bonding I've ever heard of."

Amanda marched past him and knocked on Brendan's door.

"I'll go in and check on him." Charley zipped past then returned in a few seconds. "He's suiting up."

The door opened and half of Brendan's face appeared, enough she could see that he was wearing his silver helmet and jacket. "Hi, Amanda."

Amanda gave Jake a smug look then returned her attention to Brendan. "This is my cousin Jake. He'd like to ask you a few questions about the aliens, if that's okay."

Brendan opened the door wider and eyed Jake askance. "I don't like him."

"That's okay. I don't like him either. But you can trust him. He's trying to help Dawson get his brother back from the aliens."

Jake moved closer to the door. "I've dealt with aliens before. I might be able to get the boy back if I knew which group took him. Can you describe them?"

Jake hadn't asked Brendan if he'd seen the people who took Grant. Instead he'd begun with the assumption that he knew Brendan had seen them and was simply asking for a description. Amanda would have to remember that technique. It could come in handy for all sorts of situations.

Brendan hesitated, pushed his glasses up on his nose and squinted at Jake. For a moment she thought he was once again going to deny having seen the kidnappers. "Three of them. Tall and short. One man was tall and one was short, and the woman was short. They were wearing disguises, but I think they were from the Alpha Centauri system. They've been taking boys to work in the crystal mines."

Jake nodded. "Tough on the boys, digging out those crystals. Would you recognize any of these creatures if you saw them again?"

"Of course I would, but they're long gone, halfway back to Alpha Centauri by now." He looked around nervously as if uncertain whether the creatures were truly gone or just lurking around the corner.

"Maybe they are and maybe they're not." Jake lifted a hand. "Could you stay here for just a minute and let me check on something?"

Brendan looked at Amanda as if asking what he should do. Maybe the two of them had bonded in an offbeat sort of way. She nodded.

"Okay," he said.

Jake strode to the apartment next door and knocked. After a couple of minutes Nick Farner opened the door. He wore only boxer shorts, his hair was rumpled, and he sported an overnight growth of dark beard. The look worked for him, especially the semi-nude body with well-defined muscles.

Brendan disappeared inside his apartment and closed the door quietly.

"Hi, Nick. Remember me? Jake, Amanda's cousin?"

Nick rubbed his eyes and yawned. "Yeah, sure. What's up, Jake, Amanda's cousin?"

"We're out of coffee. Just wondered if we could borrow some."

"Okay." Nick disappeared back into the apartment and returned shortly with a plastic bowl containing something dark. "Here you go."

Jake accepted the container. "Thanks."

"Sure. Anytime." Nick closed the door.

Jake came back over to Amanda. "Where's our witness?"

Charley darted through the door of 3C and back again. "He's standing on the other side."

"He closed the door," Amanda said. "What did you expect? Don't you think it was a little rude to leave him like that and go borrow coffee from a neighbor right in the middle of a conversation?"

"That neighbor just got out of prison, and he is definitely not Mrs. Lowell's grandson. I wanted Matthews to see him, maybe identify him as one of the kidnappers." Jake knocked on Brendan's door.

Before Amanda could digest that last bit of information, the door opened a crack. "That's him," Brendan whispered. "That's the tall Alpha Centaurian who took the boy."

Chapter Eleven

Amanda gulped. She'd been staring at a kidnapper-murderer, thinking he had a hot bod. So much for her survival instinct. But Brendan had said there were three aliens, two men and one woman. "The short man, was he bald?" Her voice came out barely above a whisper.

"Of course. Alpha Centaurians don't have any hair. That one you just saw in that apartment over there was wearing a wig."

"What about the woman who took the boy? Was she wearing a wig too?" Jake's voice was firm and strong. Well, he was accustomed to talking to murderers and nut cases. With the exception of Charley's ghost, she usually talked to normal people.

"Of course," Brendan said. "They know earth women are never bald. She was wearing a short blondish wig. It was ugly. But I guess if you're not used to having any hair at all, you don't know what looks good and what doesn't."

"That makes sense," Charley said.

None of it made sense to Amanda, but Jake showed no surprise at Brendan's strange description.

"Besides the bad wigs, what else can you tell me about the short man and woman? Any distinctive features?"

Brendan frowned and shook his head. "It was dark. Besides, what difference does it make? They change shape at will."

"Good point. Can you tell me what time this occurred?"

"Twelve minutes and nine seconds after three o'clock this morning."

Jake didn't question the precise time. "Thank you," he said. "You've been a big help."

"Do you think the others are still on earth like that guy across the hall? Maybe they're waiting until they have a bunch of boys to take back with them. Do you want me to go to Dawson's apartment and help him set up a protective field? If they took his brother, they'll try to modify his brain so he doesn't remember he ever had a brother."

Jake cleared his throat. "We'll get back to you on that. Things are a little hectic right now."

With a nod, Jake turned toward Dawson's door. Amanda knew she should follow, but she felt glued to the spot, unable to stop staring at the strange little man. He had actually witnessed the kidnapping, but his brain was so scrambled, he saw them as creatures from another star system. Still, it was the best information they had so far.

Jake took her arm and guided her firmly away.

Brendan's door closed softly.

When Amanda and Jake returned to Dawson's apartment, they found him still focused on one of the laptops, a fresh can of Red Bull on the table beside him. "Did you find any shoe prints?" he asked without looking up.

"Shoe prints?" With the startling new development that Nick was involved in the kidnapping, Amanda had forgotten all about the silly story she'd given as an excuse to get Daggett out of the apartment. "No, no shoe prints."

"But I have some news." Jake sat down at the table.

Dawson paused with his fingers still on the keyboard. "News?"

"About Nick Farner. He isn't Mrs. Lowell's grandson, and he just got out of prison three weeks ago. Mrs. Lowell's real grandson was in the same prison. They knew each other, so the grandson probably told Farner about his grandmother."

"What was he in for?" Amanda asked. "Kidnapping? Murder?"

"Drugs."

"Drugs?" She thought of the body she'd been ogling before she knew he was an alien kidnapper. "That man uses drugs?" Maybe she could get hold of some of whatever he was taking.

"He's supposedly reformed. Got a job as a personal trainer at a local health club." He paused and looked from Dawson to Amanda. "At the Fitness 4 You Club."

Dawson's fingers ceased moving over the keyboard. His eyes widened and he shot up from his chair. "That's the place where they want me to take the program. He's got Grant! That wasn't his cat who screamed yesterday. It was my brother!"

Jake was on his feet just as quickly, placing a restraining hand on Dawson's arm. "He wouldn't be keeping your brother in his apartment. It's too close. Besides, that picture was definitely not taken in his apartment."

Dawson tried to tug free of Jake's grasp. "But he knows where Grant is."

"Probably. But if you confront him now, we'll lose any chance we have of following him and finding your brother."

Dawson ceased struggling. "If he doesn't have Grant with him, how do you know for sure he's involved?"

"Turns out your neighbor with a penchant for aluminum foil actually saw the kidnappers and identified Farner."

"What? Why didn't he tell us before?"

"Sit down." Jake spoke firmly.

Dawson sank back into his chair.

"Your neighbor is a little confused. He thinks aliens took Grant. But with what he told us, we've got a description of the other two kidnappers. We already have a description of their vehicle from Amanda and the lady downstairs, so all we have to do is keep track of Farner to see if he'll lead us to your brother."

Dawson nodded slowly, reluctantly.

"Ross will be here this afternoon. He's in the lab right now analyzing what he got from Grant's room. Between the two of us—"

"Three," Amanda corrected.

Jake ignored her and fixed his gaze on Dawson. "We can watch Nick, and I can get a warrant to eavesdrop on him. However, getting that warrant will take time."

Charley settled in the empty chair, put his feet on the table and smiled. "That's where I come in. I can eavesdrop on anybody I want to without being seen. What's the law going to do to me anyway? Put me in jail?" He laughed at his own joke.

"We don't have time," Dawson said quietly. "I can use technology to eavesdrop on him."

Poor Charley. Trumped by a computer.

"You know I can't condone your doing that," Jake said, his voice just as quiet.

"You can't stop me."

One corner of Jake's mouth tilted upward in half a grin. "No, I can't. I'm going to the station to see what Ross has found and I'll try to contact Mrs. Lowell's grandson to see what he knows about Nick."

A horrible thought occurred to Amanda. "So if this guy isn't her grandson, what's he doing in her apartment?"

"We don't know the answer to that question at this point."

He might not know, but she'd be willing to bet he had some thoughts on the subject. "What about Mrs. Lowell? Where is she? Is she really on a cruise?"

"We don't know," he repeated. "I haven't been able to find her on any passenger lists, but we can't jump to conclusions. Not finding her yet doesn't mean she's not on a cruise somewhere."

"Doesn't mean she is. Maybe they kidnapped her too. Or killed her so they could plant this guy in her apartment to keep an eye on Dawson and make sure he doesn't call the cops." Amanda shivered at the thought of the elderly lady's body still being somewhere in her home, right across the hall from where they stood.

"I didn't see her body in the apartment," Charley said. "But I didn't check for blood stains."

Amanda did not feel reassured.

"We have no reason to believe anything's happened to Mrs. Lowell." Jake used his reassuring cop voice which made Amanda think he probably did have reason to believe that very thing. "I'll let you all know what I find. Dawson, you let me know if you learn anything about Farner. I agree that they probably planted him here to keep an eye on you, so I don't think he'll leave just yet. But if he does, let me know immediately."

"If he leaves, I'll follow him," Amanda said.

"After you call me and tell me which direction he's going."

"Of course." She tried to look sincere.

Jake studied her a moment. "Do you have the GPS activated on your cell phone?"

"I don't know." Amanda took the phone from her purse.

Dawson held out his hand. "Let me see."

She handed it to him.

He frowned as he looked at the display. "Your mother's called you five times."

"Yeah, I know. She wants to talk about a baby shower I'm giving for my sister that I have no part in except lending my name. I'll call her back later. This is more important." Watching the weeds grow along the highway was more important than that silly party.

Dawson tapped through some screens Amanda hadn't known existed on her phone. "Now your GPS is activated." He handed it back to her.

She looked at the small rectangular object and then at Jake. "So you can find me through this?"

"If I have to." Jake started out the front door then paused and looked back at her. "Don't make me have to."

"If I get lost, I'll find my own way home by tracking the North Star even if it's high noon." She returned her attention to Dawson. "What can I do to help you with whatever it is you're doing on these computers?"

The door closed behind Jake.

"Forget the computers right now. I need to borrow your bike," Dawson said. "Mine's still at your shop."

Amanda studied her young friend. He didn't look so young at that moment. "Why? Where do you want to go?"

"If I'm to adequately monitor Nick Farner's activities, I need some electronics and I don't have time to order them from the Internet. I'll have to go to a brick and mortar store."

Amanda shook her head. "Go take a shower, shave, change clothes, and I'll consider letting you ride on the back of my bike."

Dawson looked startled. "I forgot about showering. Do I smell bad?"

"Bad enough you can't ride on my motorcycle until you're clean."

He nodded and headed obediently for the bathroom.

Amanda sat down at the table and looked at the three laptops. What if none of them held the program the kidnappers wanted? What would happen to Grant? What would happen to Dawson? He was on the verge of losing it. One more Red Bull and he was likely to go flying around the room alongside Charley.

She turned the nearest computer to face her and ran a finger over the touch pad to wake the screen display. Judging from the number of game icons, this was probably Grant's, maybe the one he'd been playing games on the night his parents were murdered. Sadness wrapped around her as she pictured the small boy from the photograph tapping on these very keys, laughing, having a good time, playing with friends. Then he lost that world and now he might lose his life.

She clicked on a musical symbol icon. They could use some soothing music. A new screen appeared and some really awful, really loud noise burst into the room. Grant must have different taste in music than she did. This was definitely not soothing. She clicked on "New Selection," but nothing happened.

"Be careful," Charley shouted, trying to make himself heard over the music. "You don't know anything about computers. You're going to mess something up."

"I know how to do one thing." She hit the "X" in the upper right corner and closed out the program. The silence was abrupt, blissful and intense. In that silence she heard footsteps going down the stairs.

She charged across the room and flung open the door.

Nick Farner was disappearing around the next landing.

"He's getting away!" Charley exclaimed. "I'll follow him as far as I can, but you need to hurry!"

Damn! The music had hidden the sound of his door closing.

Amanda spun back into the room and down the hall to the bathroom. "Dawson!" she shouted, trying to make herself heard over the sound of the shower. "I've got to go! Nick's leaving!"

Dawson didn't respond.

Nick was getting farther away every second and Charley was restrained by the length of that invisible leash so he could only follow the man so far.

She grabbed her jacket, helmet and keys and ran out the door. She'd call Dawson when she got a chance. And Jake. Okay, she'd sort of agreed to call him *before* she left to follow Nick, but she didn't have time. Exigent circumstances.

Chapter Twelve

"There he goes." Charley pointed to a beige Honda pulling out of the parking lot.

"Keep him in sight. I'll be right behind you." Amanda shoved on her helmet, revved the engine on her bike and pulled out, heart pounding wildly. This could be it. Nick could be heading straight for the place where Grant was being held. Too bad she'd left her .38 at home, but when they got to the kidnap site, she could call Jake. He and Ross would rush over with their guns and rescue Dawson's brother.

Following Nick across town proved surprisingly easy with Charley flying between them, signaling turns. Of course she could have done it just fine without him.

Nick seemed oblivious to them. He drove in a totally normal manner, making no effort to evade potential followers. Apparently he thought his ruse was working, that they were too dense to catch on. What incredible arrogance. Taking him down would be gratifying.

He drove straight to Fitness 4 You and pulled into the lot behind the spa.

Amanda parked her bike several spaces away and watched him walk into the employee entrance. She pulled off her helmet and looked at Charley. "Maybe he's just going to work."

"No! He probably doesn't even really work here."

"Jake said he does."

"What does Jake know? It's all a cover. The kid's probably inside that place and Nick's going in to torture him. Cut off a finger like they threatened."

Amanda shivered. "Stop that! We have until 6:00 before they start sharpening the knife. Maybe he's going to work as usual so he can keep an eye on the locker and tell the others when Dawson brings the program. We may be wasting our time watching him watch the locker. He may not be going anywhere near Grant."

"You just sit here and relax, read a book or something while I go inside and see what he's up to."

"You think I'm going to relax? I am not going to relax until this is over. But go ahead. If I go in, he'll spot me. At least he won't recognize you." Amanda unstrapped her purse from the sissy bar and took out her cell phone. "I'll call Dawson and tell him why I ran out on him."

He answered on the first ring and she explained what had happened. "I don't think they'd be keeping Grant here, but maybe Farner will do something or call somebody. I'll let you know as soon as I find out what he's up to."

"Thanks, Amanda. I feel better just knowing we're doing something."

Dawson's gratitude and trust intensified Amanda's need to do something productive, and sitting in the parking lot waiting for Charley didn't seem very productive.

Nevertheless she pulled off her leather jacket, draped it over the handlebars and waited.

Thirty minutes later Charley had not returned and the day wasn't getting any younger or cooler. Even in her cotton shirt, Amanda was starting to sweat. She had a couple of choices. She could go into the fitness club and search for a ghost or she could ride away. If she did the latter, Charley would have to follow once she'd gone a certain distance and then she could ask him what he'd seen.

But what if Nick left while she was dragging Charley away?

She sighed and climbed off the bike. She had to go inside and find out what Nick and Charley were doing. Surely Nick hadn't figured out a way to hold Charley captive. If he had, she could only hope he'd keep him for a few decades.

However, if Nick saw her and recognized her, he'd know they were on to him. She could wear her helmet and avoid recognition but she'd most certainly be noticed. Leave the helmet strapped on the bike, throw the jacket over her shoulder and keep her head down. A search through her motorcycle bag yielded a scarf she hadn't worn since winter. She wrapped it around her head, hiding her red hair. Not the best of disguises but it would have to do.

She walked up the front steps and through the entrance then stopped to look around.

Charley was easy to spot. He hovered a few inches from a young, gorgeous blonde who was being guided through a workout by Nick. Charley's journey to the other side might have stopped him from lying but apparently it hadn't stopped him from lusting.

Amanda stood for a few moments watching the three. She hadn't needed the disguise after all. Nick didn't so much as glance in her direction. He was completely involved in his work. However, so was Charley. She could think of no way to get his attention without getting Nick's at the same time.

She'd have to fall back on Plan B, ride away, eventually yanking him from the building and the vicinity of the blonde. It was probably safe to leave Nick alone for a while since he seemed as enthralled with his job as Charley was.

She turned and went back outside.

Her cell phone rang as she reached her bike. Her mother again. As if she didn't have enough on her plate what with trying to find Dawson's brother and deal with an over-sexed, psychotic ghost. The freaking shower invitations would have to wait. She shoved the phone back into her bag and couldn't stop herself from making a comparison. Sunny would never obsess over something as silly as a baby shower. Sunny had her priorities straight.

She jumped on her bike and peeled out of the lot.

Charley appeared in front of her about three blocks away, waving his arms and trying to get her to stop. When she pulled up to a red light, he confronted her. "What are you doing? I thought we were supposed to be watching that guy."

"You were supposed to report to me as soon as you saw what he was up to."

131

Charley rubbed the back of his neck and looked away. "I was waiting for him to finish the workout with that woman. I mean, it's not like he was going to stop in the middle and go do something else."

"And it's not like I'm going to sit in the hot sun all day and wait for you to report back to me when we're on a tight deadline to find Grant." A car horn sounded behind her. The light had turned green. She twisted the handlebar grip and rode away.

༺ঌ

"We need to go back," Charley insisted as he followed Amanda up the stairs to Dawson's apartment. "We need to keep an eye on that guy."

"Ha! You just want to keep an eye on his female clients."

"Are you jealous, Amanda?"

"Oh, Charley, it's been a very long time since I've been jealous of your bimbos." She rounded the second floor landing and smiled. "Besides, now all you can do is look. You can't touch."

"You can be a cruel woman, Amanda."

She probably ought to stop talking to him. Anybody seeing her would think she was having a conversation with herself. Not that there was anybody on the third floor to see her except Dawson or the aluminum foil guy. She took the last flight of stairs as quietly as possible so Brendan wouldn't hear her and come out again to zap aliens with his laser gun.

That effort proved unnecessary. When she entered Dawson's apartment she saw aluminum foil covering the windows and Brendan sitting at the table with Dawson. The tinfoil guy looked up when she came in. "I want to help protect him from the aliens."

She gave Dawson a lifted eyebrow, *What the hell?* look. He shrugged as if the man's presence there was inconsequential.

Had Dawson become so desperate he would accept help no matter how off-the-wall that help was?

Apparently.

"Thanks, Brendan," she said, "but we can handle it. My friend, the one you met this morning, he and his partner—I mean, his co-worker—are experts in dealing with aliens, and they'll be here soon."

"They don't have my shield program."

He indicated a laptop sitting on the table, and Amanda realized there were now four of them. They were multiplying.

"I wrote the program," he continued, "and I'm the only one who has it, but I'll share with Dawson because I know he's not one of them since they took his brother too."

"Too?"

Brendan nodded so vehemently his thick glasses slid partway down his nose. He pushed them back up. "They took my brother and me, but I escaped. That's how I know so much about them. I can put up cyber shields as well as physical shields to protect Dawson."

She looked at Dawson who again gave a slight shrug. Brendan was probably a harmless nut. But at this point they didn't need any distractions or outside influences, even harmless ones. "Dawson, I need to see you in Grant's room for a minute. I have a question about one of his posters."

"His posters?"

"Yes." She headed toward Grant's room.

"I'll keep an eye on metal man," Charley called.

Amanda continued down the hall to the second bedroom. She was dealing with a ghost, a guy who saw aliens and wore tin foil, and a stressed-out kid who was so desperate he was willing to consider alien protection provided by a nut job. She was the sanest one of the group. That was a scary thought.

Dawson entered Grant's room behind her, and she closed the door. "Aliens did not take your brother, that guy is not going to be able to help, and we don't need him here in the middle of things right now."

Dawson shook his head. "I know he's a little different, but he did see the kidnappers. Maybe he and his brother really were kidnapped, not by aliens, but by the same people, and maybe he did escape, and maybe he knows something about them that will help us."

Amanda looked at her friend, at the lines on his face, lines that hadn't been there two days ago. "I know you're under a lot of stress right now. I can't even begin to imagine how upset you must be."

Dawson moved over to Grant's bed and sank down, picking up the stuffed dog and holding it to his chest. "My brother's the only family I've got. I moved to a city where I didn't know anybody, and I've been afraid to make friends because I was afraid to trust anybody. It's just been Grant and me for two years and now he's in trouble and I don't know how to help him."

Amanda sank onto the bed beside him. "We're going to find him. You're going to get your brother back. And you do have a friend...me. When this is over, you're going to make lots more friends. As far as family, I'll be happy to share mine with you. What with birth family, adoptive family, and in-laws, I've got more than enough to share. Off the top, you can have my sister and my mother."

Dawson gave a small hiccup of a laugh. It was better than nothing. "Thanks, but I think I'll pass on both of them. Right now having Brendan here makes me feel more secure. He knows a lot about computers. We talk the same language. And he saw the people who took Grant."

"What the heck," Amanda said, giving in. "If it makes you feel better, I suppose one more crazy person around here won't matter."

To her surprise, Dawson leaned over and gave her a quick hug. "I appreciate all you're doing to help, Amanda. You are my friend." He stood and left the room.

A warm spot settled in the middle of Amanda's chest, a warm spot that had nothing to do with the broiling temperatures outside. If having the goofy little man there made Dawson feel better, she'd do her best to keep him there and see that he didn't cause any problems.

She followed Dawson back to the living room.

"He did something with Dawson's computer!" Charley said. "I tried to stop him, but I couldn't! My hands just went right through him! Don't ever die, Amanda. It's not as much fun as you might think."

Chapter Thirteen

So much for Brendan being harmless. Amanda charged over to where he sat. "What did you do to his computer?"

Dawson gaped at her in surprise. Brendan blinked rapidly behind his thick glasses. He swallowed, his Adam's apple bobbing. "I was just looking."

"Looking at what?"

"I—I wanted to be sure he has enough RAM for my program to run."

Dawson glanced down at his laptop then back up to Amanda. "How did you know he was on my computer? He wasn't when I came back to the room, and you were behind me."

Both men stared at her, waiting for an answer. She looked from one to the other.

Charley laughed. "Time to acknowledge your husband's help."

Amanda hovered a hand about an inch above the keyboard of Dawson's computer, moving it back and forth. "I can feel the energy from his fingertips."

Dawson put his hand beside hers. "Really? That's amazing. I can't feel anything."

"It's a talent. Inherited from Grandmother Phoebe."

Dawson frowned. "That's your mother's mother and she isn't related to you by DNA."

"Yep. That's why the talent's so strange. Look at the time. Why don't I go pick up some lunch? You boys carry on with whatever you're doing."

She grabbed her helmet, jacket and purse and dashed out the door.

Of course Charley followed. "Don't leave him alone with that nut. I don't trust him. He was doing a lot more than checking for RAM on Dawson's computer."

Amanda laughed. "How would you know what he was doing on the computer? You think RAM is a male sheep."

"I know about computers. I can go inside them and make the pictures do wonky things. You can't do that."

Amanda rolled her eyes. Arguing with Charley was a waste of time and energy.

Her cell phone rang. "Oh, not my mother again." But this time it was Sunny. Amanda answered as she walked down the stairs.

"Your mother's on a rampage," Sunny said.

"Which mother?"

Sunny laughed. "The one who goes on frequent rampages. Seriously, Amanda, she's worried about you. You haven't been answering her calls, and your shop's closed."

"She went by my shop?"

"She's worried. She called Irene and me to see if we'd heard from you."

Amanda pushed through the outside door into the midday heat. "I hope you told Irene there's nothing to worry about." She'd already given her mother-in-law plenty of reason to worry a couple of months ago when she'd stayed with her while trying to prove Roland Kimball was a murderer. The first woman who'd ever baked cookies for her—other than her mother's various cooks, of course—deserved some peace of mind.

"I told Irene and your mother that I saw you yesterday and we had an uneventful motorcycle ride."

"Thank you for not telling them about the kidnapping. I don't want to upset Irene or give Mom so many gray hairs she has to run to her hairdresser. Remember those strange people in the van who were following us? They may have been Grant's kidnappers." As she walked around the building and over to her motorcycle in the parking lot, Amanda updated Sunny on the latest developments.

Sunny was silent for a long moment. "You followed a guy who just got out of prison? Do you think it was a good idea to follow a known criminal and spy on him?"

Amanda hesitated. She considered telling Sunny that Charley had actually done most of the following and spying, but after the disaster yesterday of trying to tell her about Charley, she decided not to revisit the topic right then. "I was never in any danger. Well, I need to run. I'm going to pick up lunch for Dawson. Can't ride and talk on the cell phone at the same time."

"Amanda, one more thing. About Charley."

Amanda looked at the ghost in question who was entertaining himself by teasing a small black dog. He darted toward the dog who barked and backed away then, wagging his tail, trotted toward Charley and rolled over to have his tummy rubbed. Her ex could never get a role in a scary ghost movie.

"What about Charley?"

He turned at the sound of his name. "Dogs and cats can see me. Maybe I'm getting more real." The dog stood up and extended a paw toward his hand.

"You said some things that concerned me." Sunny's voice was quiet. Worried.

"Can we talk about this another time? It's okay. I'm perfectly sane. Well, as sane as I've ever been."

Sunny laughed softly. "Okay, we'll talk later. Just be careful and remember I'm here when you need me. And please call your mother before she drives us all crazy."

Amanda disconnected, shoved the phone in her jacket pocket then sighed and took it out again. She dialed her mother's number and breathed a sigh of relief when the call went straight to voice-mail. "You've reached Beverly Caulfield's phone," her mother's slow, precise voice informed her.

Amanda drummed her fingers on the seat of her bike as she waited for the message to finish and get to the beep. Too bad there wasn't a way to fast forward through messages longer than ten words. Amanda's own was, *This is Amanda. Leave a message,* and she was thinking about taking out the *This is Amanda* part.

"I'm not available at the moment," her mother's voice continued, "but if you'll leave a message, I promise I'll call you back at my first opportunity. In the meantime, I hope you have a wonderful day."

"Hi, Mom. It's Amanda Caulfield. Dad probably told you that's my official name these days. You can put it on the invitations or leave it off. Just don't put Amanda Randolph on them. Do whatever else you think needs to be done. You have proxy for my vote. My shop's closed because I'm taking a few days off. Hanging out with friends. Learning new uses for aluminum foil. Bye." That should keep her mother happy for a while, thinking Amanda was doing something that involved making cute little decorations using aluminum foil. Anything was more acceptable in her eyes than motorcycle repair.

 ⁖⁖ 

Almost an hour later Amanda made it back to Dawson's apartment with a couple of boxes of chicken and French fries strapped to the sissy bar on her bike. She swept the kick stand down with a savage motion, climbed from the bike and yanked off her helmet. "What did you think you were doing? Why did you make all the chicken go stone cold so they had to fry up another batch?"

"I didn't do it on purpose. It looked and smelled so good, I just wanted to see if I could taste it, and you know what, Amanda? I could. Almost. It was almost like eating. Surely you don't begrudge me a little taste of fried chicken after all these months of having nothing to eat or drink."

"If we go to a winery, are you going to dive into one of the barrels and stop the fermentation process with your cold just so you can have a taste of wine?"

"Would that be red wine or white wine?"

"Amanda, who are you talking to?"

She gasped and whirled around to see Jake and Ross watching her from a few feet away. "How did you get here?"

Ross arched a dark brow and indicated the faded blue sedan parked at one end of the lot. "We drove in that. Just like yesterday."

Jake studied her, his forehead creasing as he squinted against the overhead sun. "We were getting out of the car when we saw you pull up. Everything okay? You sounded a little upset just now."

"Everything's fine." Yeah, everything was just fine if you didn't consider the fact that she couldn't go anywhere without her psycho ex-husband's psycho ghost. "I bought chicken." She turned and began removing the straps that held the food to her sissy bar. Perhaps fried chicken could distract them from trying to figure out what she meant when she'd asked the apparently empty air about stopping the fermentation of wine.

"Smells great," Jake said.

"It really does," Ross agreed. "I just ate, but I think I could still manage a piece of chicken."

"See?" Charley darted past her. "Either of them would have done the same thing I did. The smell of fried chicken is irresistible."

"Let me carry that for you." Jake took the sack from her as she struggled with balancing the food and her helmet.

"And I'll take your helmet," Ross offered.

"You two are such gentlemen." And, fortunately, easily distracted from the subject of her conversation with a ghost.

Charley snorted.

"So how's Dawson doing?" Jake asked as they headed toward the front of the building.

"Oh, yeah, I probably should warn you. Brendan came over while I was following Nick, and by the time I got back, he and Dawson had bonded and put aluminum foil on all the windows."

Jake and Ross both came to an abrupt halt.

"Aluminum foil on the windows?" Ross repeated.

"You were following Nick?" Jake asked.

"You're in trouble." Charley sounded delighted.

"I'll explain on the way upstairs." Amanda continued to the front door of the building.

As they climbed the steps, she told them about following Nick to work and about Brendan.

"He shouldn't be looking at Dawson's computer," Jake said. "We don't want him possibly messing up whatever's on there. I wish you hadn't left them alone."

"See how it feels when you make one little mistake and get chewed out about it?" Charley's words were a cold breeze in her right ear.

"At least I didn't freeze the chicken."

"What?" Jake asked.

143

"I said, I had to go get the chicken." She stepped onto the third floor landing and over to Dawson's door then knocked loudly.

Dawson opened the door. His eyes were still bloodshot, and he was still twitching from the Red Bull. However, he looked marginally better than she'd seen him look over the past two days. Maybe Brendan was having a positive effect on him. "I'm glad you're back. Brendan's helping me search for the program."

Amanda cringed. "You told him?"

"I didn't know what else to do. We need all the help we can get." Dawson bit his lip. "We're running out of time. Brendan's brilliant with a computer." He stepped back to allow them to enter. "Brendan, this is Amanda's cousin Jake and his friend Ross."

At least he hadn't told Brendan that Jake and Ross were cops.

"Hi, Brendan," Amanda said. "What's up?"

From his seat at the table in front of one of the laptops, Brendan regarded her solemnly. "Dawson's in grave danger. The aliens murdered his parents and stole his brother. Dawson's the only surviving heir to the throne of the entire Alpha Centauri star system."

Dawson shrugged and looked a little abashed, but the corners of his mouth tilted upward in a small, tentative smile. That smile cinched it for Amanda. If the tin man could help Dawson get through this, she was all for him.

"I brought some fried chicken. Would you like to join us for lunch?"

"Are you crazy, Amanda?" Charley demanded. "I can't believe you invited that nut to eat with us. We need to get him out of here, not feed him."

Jake said nothing, but as he plopped the boxes of food in the middle of the table, he gave her a look that echoed Charley's words.

Amanda found paper plates in the kitchen and passed them around while Dawson returned his attention to one of the computers on the table. She put a drumstick and fries on the plate beside his laptop. "Eat."

"I'm not hungry." He picked up his Red Bull can and tilted it to his lips, tipped it all the way, then frowned and slid his chair back.

"If you want another Red Bull, you have to eat first."

Again her commanding tone worked. Without protest Dawson picked up the drumstick.

While everyone except Charley ate, Brendan talked, telling a convoluted, rambling tale of evil aliens who forced Dawson's parents to flee to earth where they killed them and now had kidnapped Dawson's brother. Amanda made no effort to pay attention to the bad science fiction story. Apparently psychoses did not make for coherent plot lines.

In the silence that followed, only crunching could be heard. Even Charley had no response to the incredible tale.

"You and your brother are the last of the line, aren't you, Dawson?" Brendan asked. "You don't have any descendants, do you?"

Dawson gulped and set down his empty plate. "Descendants? No, no descendants. Grant was my only family." The color drained from his face. "I mean, *is*. Grant *is* my family."

"Of course he is." Amanda stood and picked up her plate then Dawson's. "Grant's your family, and he's going to be home with you soon." She tried to make her tone firm, ordering him to believe just as she'd ordered him to eat.

Jake rose also and picked up his and Ross' plates. Amanda added Brendan's to her stack and started for the kitchen. Jake followed.

He opened the pantry door, lifted the lid of the trash can and dumped his plates inside then held it for Amanda. As she approached, he moved closer, so close she could feel the heat from his body. Was her heart beating faster? Of course not!

He moved his lips so close to her ear she could feel his warm breath. Her heart was definitely beating faster. "If you don't get rid of that nut job, I will, and I won't be nice about it," he whispered then turned away and went back to the living room.

"You thought he was going to whisper sweet nothings in your ear, didn't you?" Charley taunted.

She glared at him and made a mental note to say something mean to him later.

"All right, folks," she said, walking into the living room and bringing her hands together with a loud clap, "time for a little after-lunch nap."

"Nap?" Dawson repeated. "We don't have time for a nap."

Amanda walked over to him and took away his latest can of Red Bull. "Yes, the prince of Alpha Centauri is going to lie down and rest for a while. He's been up all night. I don't care if you sleep or not, Dawson, but you need to rest." How many times during her youth had she heard that speech from her mother? "Brendan, you can come back over after the prince has his nap."

Brendan rose uncertainly. Amanda put her hand on Dawson's shoulder to keep him from rising too.

"Thanks for the chicken, Mrs.—uh—Amanda."

Yeah, she was obviously sounding like a bossy mother.

Brendan looked at Jake and Ross who made no effort to stand or to explain why they were staying when he had to go.

"My cousin and his friend are going to watch over Dawson while he takes a nap so the bad men from Alpha Centauri can't hurt him."

Brendan shrugged and looked at Dawson. "I'll come over later and bring some shielding material for your walls. Hang tight, buddy."

Dawson gave him a thumbs-up. "Thanks."

Jake opened the door for Brendan to leave, closed the door behind him then held a finger to his lips until they heard the soft sound of Brendan's door closing.

"Why did you do that?" Dawson demanded. "Why did you make him leave? He was helping."

"We have some things to talk about that he doesn't need to hear." Jake turned one of the deadbolts on the door then came back to the table.

Amanda took the chair next to Dawson and laid her hand over his. "You do realize that guy's talking crazy."

Dawson scowled. "Of course I know that. But he's very knowledgeable about computers. He knows as much as I do. That means we can search twice as fast."

Jake ran a hand through his hair and shook his head. "You've been running and hiding from people for two years, and suddenly you trust a nut job?"

Dawson looked at Amanda. "I trusted her and that worked out. Then she forced me to trust you and Ross."

Amanda grinned. "So what's one more nut job, huh?"

"I didn't mean it like that."

Amanda patted his hand. "It's okay. I get it. You need all the help you can get right now."

"Yes, I do. I think Brendan's okay. I mean, he can't be involved with the kidnappers because he's too...um...unstable."

Jake nodded. "I guess that's one way to look at it, but I'm not sure you want to let someone so unstable have access to your computer right now."

Dawson bit his bottom lip and drew in a deep breath. "Noted. But we only have five hours until they start—" he swallowed— "until they start taking off Grant's fingers."

"We're working some leads," Jake said. "I'm going to Dallas Regional State Prison to meet with Steven Lowell, the real grandson, at two o'clock and see what I can find out about Nick Farner."

"I'll go with you," Amanda said.

Jake's square jaw became more square. "No, you won't."

She didn't bother to argue. There was nothing to argue about. He couldn't go in as a strong-arm cop because Steven Lowell might tell Nick Farner. He needed her as part of his cover whether he realized it yet or not.

Ross leaned back in his chair and folded his arms. "And I have some information. I spent some time with Hannah from next door."

"He took her to lunch," Jake said.

Amanda raised an eyebrow. "You're dating her?"

"No," Ross said. "Of course not. I'm investigating her."

Jake snorted.

"I thought we decided she and her roommate weren't involved," Amanda said.

"Remember those long blond hairs I found in Grant's room? I needed to get a sample of Hannah's hair so I could do a DNA match to rule her out."

Jake rolled his eyes. "Not even going to ask how you managed to get a sample of her hair at lunch."

Ross grinned. "And I'm not going to tell you. Get your own techniques, buddy."

"The hair," Amanda reminded them impatiently. "What were the results of the DNA test?"

"It's a match."

Chapter Fourteen

Amanda looked from Ross to Jake, trying to discern their thoughts. "So Hannah's a suspect after all?"

Ross' expression remained neutral. "There's some evidence to suggest that, but my gut tells me she's not."

"I don't think that's your gut doing the talking," Jake said. "How does your gut explain the license plate, the hair and the fact that she's a member of the Fitness 4 You Club?"

"That's a lot of evidence against her," Dawson said.

"She was not the woman Sunny and I saw in the van," Amanda said, "and she doesn't fit the description Brendan gave us of the woman involved in the kidnapping."

"We don't know there's only one woman." Jake frowned and shook his head. "Seems like everything we learn makes this case more complicated instead of less."

"Hannah admitted she knows Grant," Dawson said. "She admitted she talked to him. He trusted her. He might have gone with her willingly." He lifted his can of Red Bull and drank, but Amanda suspected he'd reached a depth of physical and emotional exhaustion that caffeine and sugar couldn't reach.

"Yes, she knew him," Jake agreed, "which means she could have hugged him and transferred a couple of hairs. Women with long hair shed a lot."

"I can vouch for that," Charley said. "I used to find long red hairs in the shower, the floor, the car, my shirts, everywhere." He heaved a deep sigh. "I kinda miss that."

Amanda turned her back on him and faced Jake. "So next we grill Steven Lowell and see what he knows about Nick and Hannah?"

"*I'm* going to interview Lowell, Ross is going to check Hannah's class and work schedules and find out where she is right now, Dawson's going to keep looking for the program, and you are going to drop by Fitness 4 You and see what our friend Nick is up to. Don't talk to him. Don't harass him. Don't try to take him down. Just look in and let me know what's going on."

"Okay." Jake was giving her busy work, something to keep her out of the game. She was going to be at Jake's interview with Lowell but there was no point in arguing with him. Instead she grabbed her gear and headed out the door. Jake's appointment with Lowell was at 2:00. If she hurried and Charley helped her, she could check in on Nick and still get to the prison in time to go in with Jake.

৯৯

Amanda pulled into the prison parking lot just as Jake was getting out of his car a few spaces away. Success.

"You don't have to thank me," Charley said. "But you can if you want to."

Amanda yanked off her helmet and started toward Jake. "Thank you," she muttered, then cleared her throat and tried again. She had to admit that Charley had helped. She'd sped over to Fitness 4 You and let him go inside to check on Nick. He'd reported that Nick was helping a "hot"—Charley's word—brunette work out. He was safely occupied for a while. Then on her way to the prison she'd avoided a ticket because Charley warned her of a speed trap ahead.

He had helped.

She cleared her throat and tried again. "Thank you, Charley." The second attempt sounded a little more sincere. Give credit where credit was due no matter how much she didn't like doing it.

"Anything for you, Amanda."

"Jake!" She hurried over to the detective.

He squinted into the sun and shook his head. "You know what? I'm not even surprised to see you."

"Good. Let's go."

"But you're not going inside with me. I got permission for one person...me...to go in."

"You can get me in as your assistant who's a specialist in interrogation techniques."

Jake blinked twice and frowned. "What? Where did you come up with that?"

"I don't know. Probably TV. Look, if they won't let me in, I promise I'll leave. But we have to try. There's no time to argue about it. We're on deadline now. A little boy's life is at stake." She turned and headed toward the prison entrance.

"He's coming," Charley said. "He looks mad, but he's right behind you. I think you're in."

In spite of her bravado, Amanda was a little surprised at the ease with which she was admitted to the prison. Jake did his part, flashing his badge and telling the guards she was his assistant. Amanda did her part by affecting an *I have every right to be here* look. Again, give credit where credit was due. She sent a silent thanks to her mother, the one who raised her and taught her to look haughty.

After going through several doors, Amanda and Jake were ushered into a large, stark visiting room with several wooden tables and chairs. Other than the size of the room and the number of tables, it reminded Amanda of the interrogation room where she'd first met Jake when he questioned her about Charley's murder. All things considered, she didn't feel completely comfortable as they took seats at one of the tables and waited for Steven Lowell to be brought to them.

Charley darted back and forth several times past the armed guard at the door. "I just need to know I can get out," he explained. "Prisons give me the willies."

Amanda made a mental note to ask him how he knew about *prisons*, plural.

"You didn't think it would work, did you?" she asked Jake. "You didn't think they'd let me in here."

"I hoped they wouldn't," Jake replied. "But I'm not surprised. This isn't exactly a high security prison."

Amanda resumed her haughty look. "It wouldn't have mattered if this was Sing Sing. The outcome would have been the same."

Before Jake could respond, another guard and a tall, well-built man wearing a white jumpsuit entered from a door across the room. The guard escorted the man in the jumpsuit over to the table where she and Jake waited, then he moved away to stand against the wall.

Jake stood and extended his hand. "Jake Daggett. Thank you for seeing me."

The man shook Jake's hand. He seemed more intimidated than intimidating. "Steven Lowell." Like Nick Farner, he appeared clean-cut and normal, not the scarred, balding hulk she'd expected to find doing time for dealing drugs. Judging from his broad shoulders and easy movements, he probably worked out too.

"This is my associate, Amanda Caulfield."

"Hi, Steven." Amanda stood but didn't offer to shake hands. Against her will, her mother's voice rang through her head. *You don't know where those hands have been.*

Lowell acknowledged her with a nod. "You wanted to talk about my grandmother?"

Jake resumed his seat in the hard wooden chair. Amanda, Lowell and Charley did the same.

"Are you aware that Nick Farner is living in your grandmother's apartment and pretending to be her grandson?"

"Yes, I know that. Nick's my friend. Grandmother got a chance to go on a cruise with her bridge club but she needed somebody to take care of her cat. Nick got paroled before me, so he said he'd stay there for a couple of weeks. She's always called him her other grandson, so we thought it would be okay if he just said he was, and then he wouldn't have to explain to anybody about this." He waved a hand around the room. "He wouldn't have to tell anybody he was an ex-con, that he'd been in here. Grandmother's kind of ashamed that I'm here." Steven smiled weakly as he concluded his story.

"He's lying!" Charley leaned into Steven's face. "I'm something of an expert on lying, and this guy is no good at it. He sounds like he's reading from a teleprompter."

Steven's story sounded logical. It covered all the bases. But Amanda tended to agree with Charley. The story sounded rehearsed and mechanical except for the part about his grandmother being ashamed of him. Having been married to Charley, she also considered herself an expert on lying, at least being able to detect when somebody else was doing it. Life with Charley had honed her bullshit meter, and it was shrieking loudly.

"Have you talked to Nick lately?" Jake asked.

"We talk often. They're pretty lenient about phone calls and e-mail in here."

"Food decent here?"

Amanda looked at Jake. Why was he asking about prison food? Did he plan to grab a quick bite while they were there?

Steven shrugged. "Not bad."

"Better than the food in Huntsville?"

Huntsville? Damn! He'd been withholding information from her!

Steven's features pinched and his face took on a guarded expression. "Yes, it is."

"Whole place is much nicer than Huntsville."

"Yes."

"So three weeks ago you got transferred up here to a cushy prison and your buddy Nick got paroled."

Steven's eyes narrowed. "How do you know all this and what does it matter? Are you with the police department?"

"I'm a friend of Dawson, the kid who lives across the hall from your grandmother. He's quite the computer whiz. He can find out anything."

Amanda watched Steven closely for his reaction to the mention of Dawson's name. She thought his pupils contracted slightly. Or maybe not. The light was too dim to know for sure. But he was definitely becoming uncomfortable with the turn the conversation had taken. Apparently this wasn't covered by his memorized script.

Steven leaned back in the chair and folded his arms across his chest in a defensive manner. "Yes, Nick and I were both in Huntsville for possession of drugs with the intent to sell. It was steroids. All the body builders use them. It's not like we're hardened criminals. So Nick got an early parole and I got sent up here. It was a good deal for both of us."

"You were arrested at the same time on the same charges. Why is Nick out and you're not?"

Steven's gaze darted around the room as if looking for an answer to that question. He licked his lips. "He had a better lawyer."

"Lying!" Charley slapped his palm on the tabletop...and through it. "He's lying and doing a terrible job of it! If anybody knows about lying, it's me." Charley paused and frowned. "That didn't come out right."

Amanda leaned toward Steven. "What cruise line is your grandmother on? So many of them seem to be having problems lately. I hope your grandmother isn't on one of those ships with problems."

Tiny beads of perspiration appeared on Steven's upper lip though the room was cool, a little chilly actually. He swallowed. "I don't know. Her bridge club had reservations for a block of rooms, and she opted in at the last minute when Nick came around to take care of Miss Kitty."

"She couldn't have boarded Miss Kitty somewhere?"

A small smile touched Steven's lips. "No, Miss Kitty is very sensitive, and Grandmother would never force her to spend the night away from home."

That was probably the second truthful thing the man had said yet.

Jake slid his chair back, the scraping sound loud in the quiet room. Steven jumped at the noise. Jake rose and again offered his hand. "Thank you for your time. You've been very helpful."

Steven Lowell stood, his movements jerky and uncoordinated, no longer smooth like the conditioned athlete he appeared to be. He shook Jake's hand, gave a phony smile and turned away. The guard came over to escort him.

Jake and Amanda walked silently out of the prison with Charley protesting the entire time. "Don't let him get away! The man's lying! You didn't find out anything from him. He totally stonewalled you."

As soon as they walked through the last door and stepped into the sunshine Amanda drew in a deep breath of the hot, thick summer air. It felt much better than the cool, trapped air of the prison. "Remind me never to commit a crime. I don't think I'd like being in one of those."

"Good idea. Maybe that should give you some incentive to try to stay out of trouble." Jake headed toward his car.

Amanda stayed with him. "You didn't tell me about the Huntsville thing."

Jake paused. "There was no reason to tell you. I didn't know you were going to be here."

"Did you notice that he never asked why we were asking all those questions? I find that very suspicious. Wouldn't you think he'd want to know why we wanted to know?"

They reached Jake's car. He stopped and looked at her. He didn't exactly smile, but he didn't frown either. "I did notice that. Very perceptive of you to notice."

Jake had sort of praised her. Amanda lifted her chin. "He was expecting us, wasn't he?"

"Right again."

"Every word out of that man's mouth was a rehearsed lie except for the business about his grandmother being ashamed of him and not sending Miss Kitty away from home."

Jake nodded. "It's not looking good for Nick."

"Not looking good for Hannah either what with the evidence Ross found. Do you think they're in it together?"

He studied her for a moment then gave an almost imperceptible shrug. "Let's talk about this in my car, out of the heat. Get some air conditioning going."

Jake was inviting her to sit in his car with him? Amanda mentally picked her jaw up off the ground. "Yeah, sure," she said casually though she didn't feel casual. She wasn't sure exactly how she felt. Pleased that he was inviting her to join him? Yes, definitely that. Also maybe a little excited. She didn't want to examine that feeling too closely.

"No!" Charley darted in front of her. "Didn't your mother ever warn you not to get in a car with a strange man?"

If only her mother had warned her not to marry a strange man.

Jake's car was parked in the sun and the air was even hotter inside than outside, but he started the engine, turned on the a/c and opened both doors. Sitting inside with the air blowing was marginally cooler than outside in the sun with no breeze stirring.

Amanda laid her jacket and helmet in the back seat next to Charley. "So Steven Lowell was expecting us."

"He was expecting somebody."

"He was prepared just in case somebody came around asking questions. Had his story memorized."

Jake stretched his long denim-clad legs as far as he could inside the car, settling his scuffed boots alongside the pedals. "A story that exonerates Nick, if we believe that story."

"I don't believe it."

"Neither do I."

"Okay, we've got Nick who's an ex-con pretending to be somebody he's not, works at the drop site, may have murdered Mrs. Lowell, and Brendan identified him as one of the kidnappers."

Jake nodded. "And Hannah whose hair we found at the crime scene, whose license plates somehow made their way to that van you saw and who's a member of Fitness 4 You."

"Then there's the man and woman I saw in the van who match the tin man's description of the other two people who kidnapped Grant." She held up four fingers. "Four people. It's possible they could all be involved."

"Possible. Nick's new to the apartment building. He could have moved in to keep an eye on Dawson and Grant. But Hannah lived there before Dawson and Grant moved in. That would have to be quite a coincidence for her to be involved."

"Sounds like Ross isn't the only one who's got the hots for the blonde," Charley said.

Amanda folded her fingers into a fist. "Coincidences do happen. That's why we have a word for them. Maybe that's how these people found Dawson. He and Grant moved into her building and Hannah told her buddies."

"Anything's possible, but that sounds unlikely."

"You think they're trying to frame Hannah to divert suspicion from Nick?"

Jake dragged a hand through his already-rumpled hair and shook his head. "Remember what Ross said about the intricate maneuvering they did with the license plate being overkill?"

She nodded. "You think this is all a big tangle to keep us from finding the truth in the middle?"

"I don't know what to think. I even ran a check on Brendan."

"Really? You think he's capable of something so..." She spread her hands. "Something so down to earth as kidnapping?"

He grinned at her lame joke. "It's possible. He's computer literate and he's managed to insinuate himself into Dawson's life. But he's lived in his apartment for nine years. He does web design work from home and has a reputation for being eccentric. He's linked to a couple of those organizations that believe we've been invaded by aliens. His whole life is on the Internet, including posts about thinking Dawson and Grant are aliens."

"Really? He's gone from thinking Dawson's an alien to wanting to protect him from aliens?"

Jake shook his head. "I don't know. He did say Dawson was a prince from Alpha Centauri. It makes about as much sense as anything else in this case. Brendan made himself right at home in Dawson's apartment, but he's agoraphobic, never leaves his own place."

Amanda frowned. "Never?"

"I can't swear to the *never* part, but he even has groceries delivered."

"Groceries and tinfoil."

Jake gave a short laugh. "Definitely tinfoil."

"So he doesn't leave his apartment, but he went to Dawson's place. He must be really determined to save him. Maybe he took a Xanax first." Amanda glanced at the clock on the dashboard and sighed. "We're no closer to finding Grant than we were before, are we? And the minutes keep ticking."

"Yes, we are. Cases don't get solved in real life like they do on TV. Nobody jumps up and confesses. We gather the evidence, one microscopic bit at a time, and those bits pile up until we finally get an answer."

"*Finally*," Amanda repeated, glancing at the clock again. "I just hope *finally* comes before they start cutting off Grant's fingers."

Jake flinched. "I wish I could promise you it will."

"Not all kidnappings end happily, do they?"

"No." His answer was soft, barely audible, but it rang loudly through the car and Amanda's heart. "Not all kidnappings have happy endings."

"What do you do when that happens?"

He faced her, his dark gaze intense. "You steel yourself to tell the family, distance yourself from it, act detached. Then you go home and have nightmares about the victims and their families."

Amanda let out a long breath. She hadn't considered that Jake and Ross might be emotionally vested in this kidnapping, too. "I really appreciate you and Ross helping like this."

Jake shrugged. "It's what we do."

"No, you don't get to minimize what you're doing. You came as soon as I called, you didn't make Dawson fill out stupid forms, you and Ross have both put in extra hours. You've gone above and beyond, and I appreciate it."

"I like Dawson. He seems like a good kid."

"He is. I wish this wasn't happening to him."

A silence fell between them, a silence that felt comfortable and tense at the same time.

"Well, I guess we'd better get back to work." Amanda leaned toward Jake as she reached in the back seat for her helmet and jacket.

He leaned toward her, his face inches from hers, his dark eyes half-closed.

Time stopped. The sounds of the car's engine and air conditioner became muffled and far away. The temperature seemed to go up several degrees.

He lifted a hand and laid it gently on the side of her face.

With no conscious effort on her part, Amanda felt herself leaning closer, her lips only inches away from his.

"Stop that!" Charley burst from the back seat, shooting through the space between them.

Amanda gasped, jumped and sat back, her heart racing.

The fact that Charley was already dead was not going to stop her from killing him.

Chapter Fifteen

As Amanda rode back to Dawson's apartment, two very different thoughts kept spinning through her mind.

Would Jake have kissed her if Charley hadn't interrupted? She was pretty sure the answer to that was *yes*. If he had, then what?

But she'd think about that later when Grant was safe. The other thought was what Jake had said...*not all kidnappings have happy endings.*

For the second time that day she rode as fast as possible, trusting Charley to let her know of any speed traps.

Trusting. That was a word she never thought she'd use in relation to Charley.

She leaned around a corner, turning down the alley that led to Dawson's parking lot. A dark mid-size sedan pulled out of the lot and headed her way. Somebody going to the grocery store or out to visit a friend.

The alley was narrow, and Amanda moved as far over as she could. When the vehicle passed her, she glanced at the driver. The small part of her brain that wasn't distracted with thoughts of Jake's kiss and the danger to Grant's life registered that he seemed vaguely familiar, but she was in the parking lot before she realized who he looked like. She brought the bike to a stop and lifted the faceplate of her helmet.

"Charley!"

"I'm right here. You don't have to shout. I wonder if I'll lose my hearing when I get old. I don't think I can wear a hearing aid."

"Who was in that car? Am I losing my mind, or did that man look like Brendan with his hair combed and no glasses?"

Charley frowned. "Not likely. As thick as those lenses are, he'd be blind without them. He wouldn't be able to drive."

"Yeah, you're probably right. Anyway, Jake said he's agoraphobic and never leaves his apartment." She put her kickstand down and prepared to get off the bike but halted midway. "However, he did leave his apartment to go to Dawson's and insinuate himself into the investigation. That's what criminals do on TV. Maybe if he takes off the glasses, he can't see the big world and loses his fears."

"I don't think that's the way agoraphobia works."

"We have to find out if that was him." She flipped her faceplate down and put the kickstand up.

"I'm getting a little tired of all this running around everywhere while I—"

Amanda revved her bike, drowning out Charley's words of protest, and sped away in the direction the car had taken. She had neither the time nor the patience for a whiny ghost.

In spite of his whining, Charley cooperated, dashing back and forth, directing her down side streets until they reached I-35E heading north. Amanda had time to begin to feel a little silly. What were the odds that Brendan was in the car they were chasing? She'd only had that one glimpse, and without the thick glasses, it was hard to be certain.

Charley should go in for a close look and let her know. Maybe he had already done that. Surely he wouldn't be continuing to follow the car if it wasn't Brendan. Or maybe he would just to annoy her. He had been upset over her almost-kiss with Jake, and he'd protested about this latest trek. His current condition prevented him from lying, but maybe he could still be a jerk and drag her all over town on a wild goose chase.

When they exited onto I-635 going west, she began to doubt her own doubts. This was the route she and Sunny had taken on their ride to Wagon Wheel Park.

Of course, there were thousands of other possible destinations in that direction.

Another coincidence?

When Charley guided her along the same exit she and Sunny had taken, a chill ran down Amanda's spine and her heart beat accelerated. Things were moving way beyond coincidence. Was Brendan or whoever was in that car heading for the place where person or persons unknown were holding Grant captive?

What a time to have left her gun at home. For sure she'd have to call Jake and ask for his help this time. Asking for help just didn't seem very romantic.

Not that there was anything romantic about her relationship with Jake.

Though he had maybe almost kissed her.

With every mile Amanda became more certain they were heading for Grant's kidnappers. He'd come this way to his baseball games, recognized the route and done his best to convey it by making the sign of holding a wheel. Dawson was right. He was a smart, brave kid. Thanks to his ingenious clue, they were going to find him.

As soon as she got to wherever they were going, she'd call Jake. She wasn't going to do anything foolish this time. Almost getting killed by Roland Kimball a couple of months before had scared her into being cautious, especially when she was unarmed.

She glanced down at her console to check her speed and noticed a red light. Low on gas. Double damn! If she stopped to buy gas, Brendan would get too far ahead of her. She'd lose him. Anyway she probably had twenty miles left in the tank—assuming the light had just then come on. She'd been intent on following Charley and couldn't remember when she'd last checked.

She had no choice but to keep following and hope she had enough gas. Walking and pushing a motorcycle while following a speeding car would not work out very well. She always carried her HOG card and knew they'd rescue her, but not fast enough.

A few miles before they reached the park, the car turned down a dirt road. It left a cloud of dust as easy to follow as Charley.

They were getting pretty far out in the country. Open fields dotted with mesquite trees and scrub oak stretched as far as she could see. She could only hope her cell phone would still get a signal. If it didn't, she'd have to ride back to civilization and call Jake.

She looked down at the low gas light. Or maybe she'd walk back to civilization.

In a mile and a half they turned down another dirt road. Amanda made mental note of the distance and direction so she could find her way back. No wonder she and Sunny hadn't been able to find the place. Even if Jake had brought out the search parties, the dogs and the helicopters, this location would have been tough to find.

The cloud of dust turned onto another road, one so rutted the car slowed to a crawl. This was her chance to make a phone call. At that speed, Brendan wasn't going to get too far away. She pulled over, yanked off her gloves and fumbled for her cell phone.

Too late. *No signal.*

She extended her arm, held the phone as high as she could above her head and got one bar. One was better than none. She punched in Jake's number and looked up, praying the signal would hold and that he'd answer.

Charley appeared in front of her, scowling. "What are you doing? Why did you stop?"

No sound came from the phone.

"Hello? Jake? Are you there?"

"You stopped in the middle of a car chase to call that...that man? What is the matter with you? Don't you care about finding Dawson's brother?"

Amanda peered up at the phone. "Jake!" she shouted. The phone was an arm's length away and the bright sun obscured her vision, but she knew what had happened even before she lowered it to peer more closely.

No bars. No signal.

She shook the phone as if that would somehow make it work.

"Amanda! Let's go." Charley waved one hand in her face, urging her forward.

"You do electrical stuff. Make this work." She extended the phone toward him.

Charley backed up. "I don't know what to do with a cell phone. It took me two hours to figure out how to turn on a television. We don't have two hours. Put that up and let's go. Brendan's going to get away."

"Just try. Touch the phone inside like you touched Dawson's computer. If that doesn't work, we'll go."

Charley heaved a long sigh then reached toward the phone. As soon as he touched it, the display came on and flashed through a couple of screens then went to her call history. The phone tried to connect to each one of her calls in order—Jake, her mother, Sunny, her mother, Jake, her mother, her mother—

It was no use. But Charley seemed to find it entertaining. He continued to move his hands up and down through the phone in some sort of crazy rhythm. "That's enough! Stop!"

Charley withdrew his hands and the phone went back to *no signal*.

Amanda considered returning to somewhere she could get a signal, somewhere she could call for assistance. Then she could turn this over to Jake and Ross. Do the sensible thing. Let them go in waving guns and wearing bullet proof vests to rescue Grant.

But it would take Jake half an hour to get there. Brendan would be long gone by then. Even if she was in the vicinity of the place where they were holding Grant, it could still take days to search the area and find him, and they only had about an hour.

"Come on," Charley urged. "The dust is going to settle and we'll lose him."

"Did you get a close look? Do we know for sure it's Brendan?"

"I looked through the window. It's him."

She could leave as soon as she knew Brendan's destination. Go back and call Jake when she had a final location. She shoved the phone into her pocket, slammed her face plate down and pulled on her gloves. "Let's go."

The dust trail was still clearly visible, and Amanda bounced along the rutted road to another turn onto a road that was marginally smoother. Much longer on that washboard road and she'd have cracks in her teeth and bruises on her butt.

Charley suddenly appeared in front of her, waving his arms frantically.

She pulled over.

"He stopped just ahead. You need to go back a little to be sure he can't see your bike. There's not much cover around here."

Amanda peered down the dusty road. The land was flat and the road fairly straight. She could make out a building a couple of hundred yards ahead. "Is that a house?"

"It's an old farmhouse. Looks like it's abandoned. That beige minivan that was following you and Sunny yesterday is parked there too."

Amanda peered more closely. She could see both vehicles. Brendan was dragging a bundle from the passenger side of the back seat of the dark car. Another man came out to help, a man with a shiny bald head, round stomach and skinny legs...the man from the van.

What were they taking out of the car? *A body?*

Of course not. She was being paranoid.

She focused on the farmhouse with its broken windows and sides so weathered no paint remained. The porch had holes, and the screen door looked rusty and torn. The picture of Grant with the gun to his head could have been taken on that porch or even inside. The ladder back chair could have been abandoned by the last resident.

It all fit.

Had she found Grant?

She flexed her fingers, noting that her hands felt damp inside her gloves.

Now what? She had to think, be cautious, make the right decision. Grant's life could depend on what she did next.

"I'm going back far enough to get a phone signal so I can call Jake."

"Amanda! No! We're here. We need to go in and rescue the boy."

"Rescue the boy? We're not even certain he's here. What if he isn't? How are we going to make them tell us where he is? Are you going to threaten them with a cold chill if they don't tell? Even if he is here, what chance do we have? There are three of them and two of us." Had she really included Charley? "Three of them, and they're murderers. Two of us, and one of us is a ghost."

"Fine. Be a coward."

"I'm trying to be smart. If Grant isn't here, Jake and Ross will be able to make those people tell where they're holding him. If he is here, they can rescue him." Amanda made a U-turn and started back the way she'd come, going as fast as she dared on the dusty road.

A hundred feet down that road her engine sputtered and died.

Out of gas.

Damn, damn, damn!

She parked the bike, took off her helmet and turned to face Charley. Though she couldn't see her own face, she was pretty sure she was about as pale as he was at that moment. She licked her dry lips. "I guess we're on our own."

"No problem. We can handle it."

Yeah, an unarmed woman and a ghost. They made quite the rescue team. But the only other option was to walk away and abandon any possibility of finding Grant. In the time it would take them to walk back five or six miles to where they could get cell phone reception, call for help, wait for that help to arrive, then return to the house, anything could happen.

"First we need to find out if he's here. If he's not, we need to find out where they've got him." She couldn't think about what they'd do when they found Grant. One crisis at a time. She looked down the road. Most of the dust had settled. "We'll have to sneak up on them from behind. If we go stalking down the road, they'll spot us. Well, they'll spot me."

Amanda moved the bike off the road and parked it behind a tree. About as well concealed as a fire engine behind a stop sign, but it was the best she could do. She put her purse, helmet, jacket and gloves behind a big rock and started off across the stubbled field.

"You sure make a lot of noise in those boots," Charley complained as Amanda's steps crunched through the dry grass and weeds.

"Jealous? Wish you could wear motorcycle boots and make noise?"

He went along silently after that.

"Are we still going in the right direction?" Amanda asked after what seemed an eternity of trekking over the uneven ground in the hot sun.

Charley shot upward, looked around, then came back. "Yep. Just keep going and you'll come up behind the house."

In death Charley was much more helpful than he'd ever been in life. But she refrained from saying so. Maybe later.

She continued to trudge across the field.

A blue jay flew overhead and emitted his shrill call of summer sun and heat but somehow the call seemed threatening.

Finally up ahead she saw the back of the weathered house with several rusty farm implements lying around half-hidden among the tall weeds. The sturdy motorcycle boots might not be the best thing for hiking across fields, but they'd probably save her from some nasty cuts going through that minefield of weeds and metal.

"Go look," she whispered to Charley as soon as they were close enough. "See if Grant's in there."

He disappeared into the structure while Amanda squatted in the weeds behind an old plow, about as effectively hidden as her motorcycle.

Charley came back almost immediately. "Brendan and the two people from the van are in there, but Grant isn't."

Amanda's heart sank. "That means they've either left him somewhere else or he's on the property but not in the house."

"It could also mean they've already—"

"No, they haven't," Amanda snapped. She could not face that third possibility. "Grant's still alive and we're going to find him." She looked around. A ramshackle barn sat a couple of hundred feet away. Closer to the house were two sheds and a mound of earth that indicated a storm cellar. "I'll check the sheds and you check the barn. It's farther away and you're faster."

"I can do that. And I'm making a note that you admitted I'm faster than you."

"Fine. You're also deader than me. Go!"

Keeping as close to the ground as possible, Amanda crept to the nearest shed. Long summer evenings were wonderful, but she could have used some early darkness to hide her movements.

Something snagged the leg of her jeans and she whirled around, adrenalin pumping, ready to die or do battle or both.

A jagged piece of metal from one of the rusted implements had caught in the denim. She reached down and tugged it away, but it gave her an idea. She could at least arm herself with something sharp.

She found a broken piece of pipe an inch in diameter and a couple of feet long. It was better than nothing.

As she crept closer on legs that felt like overcooked spaghetti, she made an effort to be quiet. That effort included not screaming when she bumped her shin on another piece of machinery hidden in the weeds.

The door to the shed was closed with a sliding bolt but didn't seem to be locked. She pressed close to the wall and slid the bolt slowly open, flinching with every crunch it made as she forced it past the rust.

When she finally got the door open a crack, she peered in and saw shelves holding an assortment of ancient tools. Not surprising there was nothing else. That bolt hadn't been moved for a long time.

She backed out and turned to go to the other shed.

Charley settled to the earth beside her. "What have you got in your hand? That doesn't look very clean. Your mother would freak out if she saw you carrying that. Put it down."

Amanda shook the pipe at him. "This is the best I can do for a weapon."

Charley flinched backward as if she might actually be able to hit him. "Great weapon. Give somebody a case of tetanus."

"Unless you've got a better suggestion, it'll have to do right now. Was Grant in the barn?"

"No."

"He's not in here either. I'll check the other shed and you check the cellar."

Charley cringed. "Not the cellar. You know I have claustrophobia."

Amanda looked at him in amazement. The sunlight bounced off his blond hair and highlighted his blue eyes, just as in life. And just as in life, he whined.

"Claustrophobia?" she repeated. "Really? The walls closing in on you? Make you feel like you can't breathe?"

He nodded.

"You can go through the walls, and you're not breathing anyway." She hesitated, not completely certain about the latter. "You're not breathing, are you?"

Charley considered the question for a moment then shook his head. "I don't think so."

"Then go check the cellar." She turned toward the second shed, remembering at the last moment to crouch and be stealthy.

The second shed held a push lawn mower—obviously not used for a very long time—and various rusted yard implements, but no small boy.

Charley darted back to her side. If they hadn't just established that he didn't breathe, she'd have sworn he was breathless. "Grant's tied up in the cellar!"

Relief washed over Amanda. They'd found him. "So he's still alive?"

"Yes. He's alive, but Dawson's in there with him and I can't tell if he's alive or not."

<u>Chapter Sixteen</u>

"Dawson?" Amanda remembered the bundle she'd seen the two men taking from the car, the one she'd thought might be a body. *Dawson*? "What do you mean you don't know if he's alive? Is he breathing? Did you see his ghost?"

"He's tied up in a chair, but he's all slumped over. I didn't stay long enough to tell if he's breathing. No, I didn't see his ghost. That's a creepy question."

Amanda had to believe that meant Dawson was still alive. She couldn't accept anything else. But any chance to leave and summon help had been taken away. They had to get Dawson and Grant out immediately then somehow get help for Dawson if he was hurt.

She looked at her watch. "It's five thirty. The deadline is six o'clock. They should be leaving here soon to check the locker and see if Dawson dropped off the thumb drive." She lifted a hand to her mouth in horror. "What am I saying? Dawson can't drop off anything if he's here!"

"Oh. Good point."

"Go back in the house and see if you can find out what's going on."

He disappeared into the house and she moved closer to the weed-covered mound as if by that effort she could somehow make contact with the captives. The wooden door that slanted along one side was rough and old, but it was solid. It would not be easy to lift.

Several moments later Charley appeared at her side. "The good news is, Dawson must still be alive. The bad news is, I know that because they're talking about killing him and Grant now."

"Now?" The word caught in Amanda's throat. "They're going to kill them now? It's only five-thirty! They gave us until six!" She knew she was being illogical. Dawson wasn't going to be delivering anything so all bets were off, but she couldn't take it in. Her friend couldn't be killed. His brother who slept with the one-eared stuffed dog couldn't be killed. Somehow she had to stop that from happening.

"Brendan knows Dawson doesn't have the program," Charley continued. "Apparently he went back to Dawson's apartment after everybody left and drugged him then he brought Dawson and all those computers out here. These people are computer nerds. They talk like Dawson does, all those funny words. They're trying to find the program, but they don't know for sure it's even on one of the computers. They're not happy, and they're arguing about what they should do with Dawson and Grant. Brendan thinks they should make one more effort to see if either of the boys can find the program, but the woman wants to kill them immediately."

Amanda shook her head in denial. "That just can't be right! It's not six o'clock yet!"

"Really? People who commit murder and kidnapping fail to keep their word, and that surprises you?"

Amanda opened her mouth to remind him how often he'd failed to keep his word and how often she'd been surprised at those betrayals. Recriminations could wait until Dawson and Grant were safe. "What do we do now?"

Charley shrugged. "Rush in and rescue the boys?"

"Right. Any idea how we go about that?"

"You rush in and rescue them, and I'll keep watch."

"Good plan." Amanda intended for her comment to sound sarcastic, but Charley was right. It came down to something that simple. She had no other choice.

Clenching the piece of pipe that suddenly seemed very small, she made an effort to swallow her fear. "Okay." The word came out a whisper. She cleared her throat and tried again. "Okay. Let's do it."

"If those people start to come out of the house, I'll whistle."

"How about you just come tell me?"

"That would work too." Charley disappeared into the house again and Amanda crept toward the cellar.

It was uncomfortably close to the back door, which, of course, made sense. If the family who'd built the place had to dash through strong winds and heavy rain to get to shelter, they needed it close. But that meant anybody who looked out the window would be able to see her creeping through the weeds.

She reached the door and laid down the pipe so she could grasp the rusted metal handle with both hands. Heart pounding, stomach clenched into a knot, she pulled upward.

Nothing happened.

Where was that adrenalin rush people were supposed to get in emergencies that enabled them able to lift cars and carry a person under each arm from a burning building?

She tugged harder and the door moved a few millimeters. When this was over, she was going to take up weight lifting. Inch by slow inch, she got the door open. Lowering it quietly to the side was almost as difficult as opening it.

She retrieved the piece of pipe then started down the steps into the musty interior. At the bottom she stopped while her eyes adjusted to the gloom. The rock wall in the back was lined with shelves holding cobwebs, dust, and Mason jars filled with unidentifiable contents, some of which were oozing over the sides.

Two people sat in front of that wall.

The boy she'd seen in the picture the kidnappers sent looked toward her, blinking in the sudden burst of sunlight from the open door. He was tied in a ladder-back wooden chair. He'd aged since the day before. His young face was gaunt and his eyes were filled with pain and terror. Amanda's heart clenched. Nobody so young should have to go through something like that.

Dawson slouched in a similar chair, also tied with a rope, his hands behind him. He must be still alive or they wouldn't have tied him up.

Anger at the people who did this emboldened her. She hurried down the remaining few steps. "Are you Grant?"

He nodded, the movement jerky.

"Are you okay?"

Another nod.

"Is Dawson...okay?"

Grant looked at his brother and shivered. "I think so. They drugged him. That man, Scott, he pretended to be his friend and then he drugged him. They're going to kill both of us."

Scott? Was he talking about Brendan? Nobody else had pretended to be Dawson's friend.

She didn't have time to think about that. "No, they won't kill you. I won't let them."

Grant made a weak effort to smile. "You're Amanda, aren't you? I knew you'd come. Dawson always said you were his friend and you could do anything."

A surge of happiness that Dawson considered her a friend washed over Amanda at the same time her heart dropped to her stomach because she had no idea what she could do to save them.

She firmed her jaw. She wasn't going to let Dawson or this small boy down.

Grant was tied with rope a little thicker than clothesline and very difficult to untie. Amanda had a knife...in the pocket of her jacket which was back with her motorcycle. Lot of good it did her now. She laid her pipe on the floor and, with fingers that trembled, fumbled with the knots that looped around Grant's body and restrained his wrists. The boy held his small hands still, helping her as much as he could. She fervently hoped she'd have the chance to hurt the people who did this before it was over.

Charley darted in. "Hurry. They're getting ready to come down here, and the woman's got a gun."

"I need a few more minutes. Distract them."

"And just how am I supposed to do that? Tap one of them on the shoulder? Yell at him?"

"What? Distract who?" Grant asked.

"Nothing. Go haunt a computer. Not you, Grant." Maybe the boy was under so much stress, he wouldn't remember the strange things she was saying.

"So all I'm good for now is making computers go wonky? No respect for the dead." Charley left through the nearest wall.

Dawson groaned. He was alive.

The first knot in Grant's ties came loose and Amanda wanted to shout with joy at the small victory. She didn't, of course. They were far from being out of there.

Even though her fingers were slick with sweat in addition to trembling, the other knots were easy after the first couple.

As soon as she freed the last one, Grant flung the ropes off and shot up from the chair to go to his brother's side. He knelt next to him and started tugging on his ropes.

"Let me do that," Amanda said. "I have experience. See if you can wake him up."

Dawson groaned again.

"Dawson, it's Grant. Can you hear me?"

Amanda squatted behind him and began twisting the knots. She'd done it before. It should be easier this time.

It wasn't. Her shaky, sweaty fingers slipped on the rope which refused to budge. How long could Charley entertain the killers with his computer tricks?

Her breathing sounded loud and harsh to her own ears, so loud she was sure Brendan and his buddies could hear her even if they were still in the house.

Grant held his brother's face between his hands. "Dawson, you need to wake up. We're in trouble, and you need to wake up now." Despite the nightmare situation, his voice was steady. He had to be terrified, but he was successfully fighting the panic.

Grant was, as Dawson had said, a brave little boy. He deserved to live to be a brave man. She ordered her fingers to relax, to be methodical about getting the knots undone.

Charley burst into the cellar. "Amanda, get out! Now! They're coming!"

Amanda thought her heart rate had peaked already, but she was wrong. "Grant, you need to leave." She tried to speak calmly, but even to her own ears her words were squeaky and tense. "Those people are coming. Get out before it's too late."

In contrast to her breathing, her fingers seemed to move in slow motion as she twisted ineffectually at the knots.

"I'm not leaving without my brother," Grant said.

Dawson moaned and mumbled. He was coming around, but it might be too late.

The first knot came loose. Amanda almost cried with relief. "We'll be right behind you. Go for help. Run. Now."

The next knot was almost free. All they needed was a few more seconds. A few more seconds and they could escape, run through the weeds, get back to the highway, call Jake and Sunny and her father and even her mother, drink a cold Coke, eat a hot pizza—

"What the hell?"

Amanda's heart sank to the bottom of her feet at the sound of Brendan's voice.

Chapter Seventeen

"Noooooo!" Grant's small form hurtled toward the three people silhouetted in the doorway. He flung himself at the bald man standing on the bottom step next to Brendan who was barely recognizable without his tinfoil and glasses.

The bald man grabbed Grant's arms, but the boy struggled, twisting and kicking, trying to get free, trying against all odds to subdue the older, larger man.

Grant was brave, but his action was foolhardy. Attacking their captors probably guaranteed they were all going to die right there in that musty old cellar. Amanda found herself strangely calm. Her hands no longer trembled. Her heart continued to race but she felt no panic, only anger at the people who'd taken this boy, drugged her friend, tied them up and stuffed them in this dark dungeon.

Though she knew the sheer idiocy of her actions, she couldn't let Grant take the defense alone. With a sigh of resignation, she gathered her energy, charged across the packed dirt floor and launched herself at Brendan.

"Amanda!" Charley shouted. "Stop that! Are you crazy?"

To her surprise Brendan fell to the floor from the force and suddenness of her attack. She had him down.

Now what?

Her father had taught her to shoot but not to fight.

Never again would she leave her gun at home, not even if she was just going to the library.

Brendan shoved her off, pushed her to the floor and started to rise. She aimed a motorcycle-booted foot at his groin. His shriek of pain told her she'd aimed true.

A gunshot echoed loudly in the small confines of the cellar and one of the jars on the back wall exploded. The sound bounced around the small space, ringing through Amanda's head. The broken jar released a noxious odor that overpowered the smell of gunpowder.

She rolled away from Brendan while he grasped his crotch and called her rude names. She lifted her head to see if Grant had been shot. The boy still squirmed in the grasp of the bald headed man, the man she'd seen the day before in the ominous beige van.

"Stop, both of you!" The mousy woman from the van stood on the second step waving a Glock as if it were a club, her finger resting on the trigger.

Jake and Ross were right. The woman didn't know much about shooting, which meant she was more dangerous with that gun than if she knew what she was doing.

"Grant!" Amanda pushed to her feet and started toward the boy but Brendan grabbed her arm. His grip wasn't strong, and she suspected he was still experiencing some pain in his groin. She certainly hoped so. "Get your hands off me, you filthy traitor, or I'll kick you again. You need to get out of the gene pool anyway." She tried to shrug him off, but he wrapped his other arm around her neck.

Charley appeared in front of her, shaking his head. "Damn it, Amanda, you never did know when to give up!"

"Give up?" She tried to push Brendan's arm away from her throat. "Are you seriously saying I should give up?"

Brendan tightened his hold on her neck. "Giving up would be a very good idea."

"He's right," Charley said. "You're in a position of weakness. That means you've got to be smart, and the first step is to lull them into believing you're defeated. Kicking the man in the balls and calling him a traitor isn't a good way to do that."

Leave it to Charley to know the proper way to work a con. Of course, that was his field of expertise.

She made a monumental effort to cease struggling for her freedom. It went against every fiber of her being, but Charley was right. The odds were against them. They had to pretend to acquiesce, bide their time and figure out how to get away.

She groped at her side and was able to touch Grant's small arm. "Stop," she said quietly. She wanted to explain the way Charley had explained it to her, to reassure the boy they weren't giving up, just making a tactical retreat. "It'll be all right." That was the only thing she dared say. It would defeat the purpose of being sneaky if she made a public announcement about their strategy.

As if he sensed her thoughts, Grant stilled. The man holding him shoved him across the room. "Get back in the chair."

Grant turned a frightened gaze toward Amanda. She nodded and tried to look confident instead of panic-stricken. He moved to the chair and quietly resumed his seat beside Dawson who had ceased groaning and sat eerily still and silent. That revved up her panic several levels.

Dawson was all right. He had to be. She couldn't panic, couldn't think about any other possibility. She had to remain calm if she was going to get the three of them out of there alive.

"I told you we should have eliminated those two redheads on the motorcycles," the bald guy said. "Where's your friend, that other woman?"

Amanda glared at the creepy guy. "That woman is my mother, and she's looking for me. She and my two friends on the police force will be here any minute. They're tracking the GPS device in my cell phone." Amanda was fairly certain the GPS device wouldn't work when she had no service, but it was worth a shot to try the bluff. Poker 101. Another skill her dad had taught her while her mother was away at social functions.

Brendan shoved her forward. "You get over there and sit down too."

Amanda stumbled, regained her balance and turned to face the villains. "I'll be happy to sit if you'll fetch me another chair."

Grant rose. "You can sit here."

The woman stepped down between the two men and waved the gun again. "She can sit on the floor."

The packed dirt floor was covered in leaves, dead bugs, mouse droppings and no telling what else. "Have you got a broom or a rug?"

The woman fired a shot just over her head. Again the sound exploded and magnified in the small space, bouncing around the room and setting Amanda's ear drums to ringing. A lot different than shooting at the range while wearing ear protection.

"Since you put it that way..." She sank to the floor, cringing as she felt a crunch. A twig or a dead roach skeleton, and that was probably a best case scenario. She smiled reassuringly at Grant. "I sit on the floor at home all the time." Of course, her floors at home didn't crunch when she sat. Or if they did, it was only from a misplaced tortilla chip.

Brendan shook his head. "What a mess."

Amanda was pretty sure he wasn't talking about the floor.

The bald man stepped closer and extended a hand toward her. "Give me your cell phone."

Amanda considered refusing but the sight of the woman waving the gun around made her decision. She reached into the pocket of her jeans and pulled it out. As soon as they saw it had no service, they'd know she'd been bluffing about the people tracking her.

She drew back her arm and threw the phone as hard as she could against the rock wall of the cellar, flinching at the shattering sound her poor phone made. Everyone including her stared at the ruins. She'd only had that phone a week, just time enough to get her contacts updated and her favorite songs downloaded, plus it was the only place she'd stored Jake's cell number.

Her hatred of those people surged to even greater heights. The loss of her phone was one more thing to add to her list of wrongs she was going to get revenge for.

She lifted her chin and stared directly into baldy's eyes. "You do not get to read my private texts or see my sexting messages to my boyfriend."

"What?" Charley shouted. "Boyfriend? Sexting? I knew you had something going with that Jake!" He paused and looked confused. "But when did you do it? I never saw any sexting messages."

Charley had been snooping on her phone. She made a note to get back to that conversation later when her life wasn't in danger.

The bald man lunged toward her. "Roger!" Brendan shouted. "Forget about the phone. It's not important."

"Scott's right," the woman said. "Get out of the way and let me shoot her."

Scott. That was the name Grant had mentioned. Brendan was Scott? She'd think about that later too. At the moment it took second place to the woman's desire to shoot her.

"Killing me would not be a good idea." She licked her lips and tried to come up with some reason why it wouldn't be a good idea other than the fact that she still had motorcycles to ride and Cokes to drink. "That boyfriend I sent those sexting messages to, he's one of the cops I mentioned."

Brendan/Scott frowned. "Neither one of those police officers acted like your boyfriend."

"You knew they were cops?"

"Of course I knew. We've had Dawson bugged for the last three days. What did you think I was doing with all that electronic equipment in Brendan's apartment? Searching the skies for aliens?"

Brendan's apartment, not *my apartment.* That didn't sound good.

"Well, Jake and I didn't make a public announcement, but he's my boyfriend all right. He spent last night at my place."

"No, he didn't!" Charley protested, then suddenly smiled. "Oh, I see. You're bluffing again. Good job, Amanda. You're getting to be a top notch con artist."

Amanda just hoped she was going to make it out of there as a live con artist.

"We need to shoot all three of them and get out of here," the woman said. "There's no reason to keep them alive now."

Amanda ducked as the woman carelessly waved the gun in her general direction.

"Alice is right," the bald man—Roger—said. "We can't stay here. The police could be on their way already if Red's telling the truth. Scott, you established that neither one of those boys knows where that program is, so they're worthless to us. We have the computers and we need to get rid of these loose ends."

Brendan was definitely Scott. But Brendan was a real person who'd lived in Dawson's building for nine years, long before Dawson's parents were killed. Jake had verified all that, and Scott had referred to the place he'd been staying as *Brendan's apartment*.

A horrible possibility reared its ugly head.

"Scott." She said the name aloud, and the man she knew as Brendan looked at her. "Where's the real Brendan?"

Scott snorted. "*The real Brendan*? Are you referring to that wimp who tried to contact aliens and allowed his phobias to trap him in that awful apartment? The only thing he was good for was helping us find these two and lending us his computer equipment."

"He helped you find them?" Jake had mentioned Brendan's Internet posts about Dawson being an alien.

"These boys aren't smart enough to hide. Dawson acted so suspicious, Brendan got paranoid and tried to track them down. When he figured out their identities were false, he decided they were aliens and posted it all over the Internet. If he hadn't done that, we might never have found them." He shrugged. "I needed to use his place to keep an eye on things and his Internet connection to send the messages. He didn't like that idea, so he's in a plastic bag in the back of our van."

Grant gasped but said nothing.

In a plastic bag in the back of their van? Amanda had never met the real Brendan, but that image clenched her gut and added to her anger. She leaned forward. "You killed a human being and stuffed him in a trash bag? You kidnapped a kid? And all for some stupid computer program? You're monsters!"

"Shut up!" Roger stepped forward and slapped Amanda so hard lights flashed before her eyes.

"Are you okay, Amanda?" Charley and Grant both asked at the same time. Charley hovered close, passing through Roger and causing the man to shiver then step back.

Amanda drew a hand over the side of her face. She didn't feel any blood but she wouldn't be surprised to end up with a bruise, maybe even her first black eye. However, she wasn't about to admit it hurt. "I'm fine. He hits like a girl."

Roger grabbed her arm and yanked her up to face him.

"Back off, Roger," Scott said quietly. "Amanda, it's not a good idea to insult somebody who has the power to hurt you."

He and Charley were on the same page with that one.

Roger released her and she fell back to the floor with another crunch. The first thing she was going to do when she got out of there was take a shower. She'd probably have to throw away the jeans.

"What about the real Nick Farner and the real Hannah Wilder? Are they in the back of your van too?"

Scott laughed, the sound closer to a snarl than honest laughter. "They're fine. No humans were harmed in the making of those smokescreens. Those two were just diversions to allow us to get away before anybody figured it out."

Suddenly all the things that hadn't made sense clicked into place. "Hannah's license plate, Nick's job at the health club, all that was your convoluted effort to mislead us, turn our attention to them so we'd ignore you. What about Mrs. Lowell? Is she on a cruise or in a trash bag in your van?"

"She's on a cruise to Alaska, a cruise we paid for."

"She's not on the passenger lists."

Scott smirked. "We write computer software. We're the best at what we do. Getting her name off the passenger lists was easy. Getting Nick Farner out of prison and Steven Lowell transferred to a better facility so we could set up that part of the diversion and have them go along with our little *joke* was more complicated, but still no problem for us. We're good."

Charley appeared next to Scott. "Play to his ego, Amanda. Encourage him to talk about what brilliant computer guys they are. Suck up to him."

Amanda looked from smug Charley to smug Scott. She didn't want to suck up to Scott. She wanted to lash out, attack him with her words since that was the only weapon she had available at the moment. Instead she gritted her teeth and forced herself to smile. "Computer software. I see. You know all about writing code and that kind of genius stuff. So why do you need that program from Dawson? Why don't you just write your own program if you're so smart?"

Scott's expression told her she hadn't succeeded in sucking up. His brows lowered and his eyes narrowed. "If Dawson wasn't so simple minded, he could find that code."

"My brother's brilliant!" Grant shouted. He wasn't any better at sucking up than she was.

Scott snorted. "I thought maybe your brother was stalling, pretending he didn't know anything about the program your father wrote. That's why I came over to check it out for myself, but he's really so dumb he couldn't find it."

Grant shot out of his chair and lunged for Scott.

Damn! Not again. Amanda leapt up and grabbed him just as he grabbed Scott. "Bad idea," she whispered in his ear. He struggled for a moment then gave up with a noise that sounded suspiciously but only briefly like a sob. She wrapped an arm around him and led him back to his chair.

Dawson still hadn't moved. Amanda glanced at Grant to see if he'd noticed. His worried gaze met hers. He'd noticed. "It'll be all right." She whispered the words again, but she wasn't sure she believed them.

"If we're finished with all the chit chat, I vote we kill them now," Alice said. "There's no reason not to. We can find the program. We don't need them." She lifted her arm, aiming the Glock in Amanda's general direction.

"Dawson knows where the program is!" Amanda shouted, trying to be heard over the thundering of her own heart.

<u>Chapter Eighteen</u>

Scott moved closer to her, pushing Alice's gun-wielding arm toward the floor. "No, he doesn't. I was there, remember? He had me help look for it. He has no idea."

Amanda twisted her lips into a sneer and forced herself to speak around the huge lump in her throat. "You really think Dawson trusted you? You really think he didn't see through your silly masquerade?"

Scott grinned. "Yes, I really think he trusted me. Dawson was ready to trust anybody he thought might help him. I became his new best friend."

Amanda snorted...derisively, she hoped. "You may be a hotshot computer nerd, but you don't know squat about people. Dawson knew where the program was the whole time. He copied it to a flash drive and gave it to Jake to take to the drop site. Jake and Ross were going to follow you when you came to pick it up. Dawson was just pretending all the time, delaying until they could get everything set up."

"That's a pretty good spur of the moment story," Charley said. "I'm impressed."

Amanda was too. Apparently terror sparked her imagination and ability to lie.

Scott folded his arms and looked down at her. "I don't believe you."

Amanda folded her arms, the action serving two purposes, to mimic and mock him and to hide her shaking. Her mouth was dry as the dirt on the road outside. She swallowed and forced the words up her arid throat, making every effort to keep her voice from wavering. "Fine. Don't believe me. That's your choice. You're going to kill us anyway. The only question is when. You can kill us now and hope you'll be able to find that program you're so hot for, or you can wait until Dawson wakes up and get the information from him before you kill us. Up to you."

"She's just trying to stay alive until her boyfriend gets here." Alice waved the gun again.

"We've got the computers," Roger said. "Shoot them and let's get out of here."

"These three will be easier to take with us if they're bodies in bags instead of jumping around and talking." Alice pointed the bobbing gun in Amanda's general direction.

"All that's true," Scott said. "But our efforts will have been for nothing if we don't find that damned program. We'll be back to square one, and that's nowhere." He looked at Dawson. "I gave him a rather large dose of zolpidem in his Red Bull and I think he drank most of it. It's got a short half-life, but he should be out at least another couple of hours. We don't dare wait that long since she says her boyfriend's on the way. We could take Dawson with us and kill the others." He arched an eyebrow in Alice's direction. "Please refrain from using your new toy on him until we're sure we don't need him."

Alice shrugged. "Okay, I'll just shoot the other two." She swung the gun around and it went off, exploding through one of the rock walls off to the side, scattering shards of stone and dust over all of them and setting Amanda's ears to ringing again. She'd probably have permanent hearing loss after this. The smell of gunpowder almost overpowered the musty scent of the cellar and the smell of rotten something that came from the broken jar. It was a little improvement.

"I didn't mean to do that." Alice smiled. "But I think I'm getting good with this thing. When this is over and we start getting our money again, I'm going to have lots of guns."

Things weren't going well. "Dawson will never tell you where the code is if you kill his brother," she threatened.

"Or his best friend," Grant added.

Scott shrugged. "We'll have to take that chance. We've got to get away from here before your cop boyfriend gets here."

Damn. Just as she'd told Charley many times, lies always come back to haunt you.

She drew in a deep breath and prepared to say the only thing she could think of to save them, however briefly. "Jake's not coming. I lost cell phone service several miles back." Her confession meant she'd destroyed her new phone for no reason.

A smug grin spread over Scott's face. "I wondered about that. We're pretty far off the grid to get cell phone reception. We lost our service back by the highway."

"That means you have time to wait for Dawson to wake up and give you the code."

"Unless you were lying about that too."

"She told the truth." Grant's voice was small but strong. "My brother knows about the program. Dad left a note telling him everything."

"Now the boy's lying," Roger said.

Scott peered at Grant as if trying to read his mind. Grant returned his gaze, never wavering. "If he's always known about the program, why was he so upset when we took you? Why didn't he just give it to us?"

"He wasn't upset. He was pretending. He knew you'd kill me just the way you killed our parents no matter if he gave you the program or not. He's been buying time to give the cops a chance to find you."

"The kid's good," Charley said. "I almost believe him myself."

Scott turned away from them, toward the door. "Roger, drive down the road and see if anybody's coming. Alice, give me the gun and let's go inside to get things ready to leave."

Alice scowled but slapped the Glock into Scott's hand. The three of them exited the cellar, letting the door close with a thud.

Total darkness filled the room, pressing against Amanda as if it were a tangible force, invading her senses with the musty scent of the underground as well as the lingering smells of gunpowder and rot or maybe it was just the lingering odor of the three beasts who'd been there.

Faint streaks of luminosity coming through small cracks in the ancient wood revealed the location of the door but didn't let in enough light to allow them to see their surroundings or even outlines of each other.

"Put something on that door so they can't get away," Scott ordered from outside.

Sounds of metal creaking and rattling were followed by heavy thuds.

As soon as the sounds stopped, Charley came through that door, frowning, completely visible, glowing faintly in the darkness. Amanda groaned. She couldn't see her own hand in front of her face but she could see him. That was just wrong.

"They laid some heavy stuff on it," he said. "I don't think we'll be able to lift it."

"*We?*" Amanda snapped. "I don't know about you, but Grant and I can lift that door."

"Get this rope off my hands and I'll help."

Grant gasped. "Dawson!"

"Dawson? You're awake? You're alive!" The last word came out of Amanda's mouth as a sound somewhere between a sob and a laugh.

"Are you okay?" Grant asked, his voice trembling. "I was afraid—"

"I'm fine except my hands and arms are getting numb. I've been awake for several minutes. I let them think I was still unconscious until I could get my hands free, figure out what was going on and attack them before they realized I was awake. But that didn't work out so well."

Amanda felt suddenly giddy. Dawson was alive and ready to help them get out of this mess. She was so happy, she wasn't even mad at Charley for being visible. Suddenly anything seemed possible. It didn't matter that Jake wouldn't be able to save her. They'd save themselves. "So you heard everything," she said. "They don't expect you to wake up for another couple of hours."

"I heard. Either that creep's better at hacking than he is at administering drugs, or all that Red Bull I drank counteracted the zolpidem. I still feel pretty wired."

Amanda rose from the floor, her balance strangely affected by the total darkness.

"Watch it," Charley warned. "Grant's up too. He's trying to get Dawson's ropes undone."

"You can see in this dark?"

"Of course I can," Charley said. "Can't you?"

"No," Dawson replied in answer to Amanda's question. "I can't see a thing."

"Neither can I, but I'll be able to get these ropes loose by feel," Grant said. "There's only a couple of knots left. Amanda already got the hard ones."

She stumbled to the back wall and made her way toward Dawson by touching the dusty, disgusting shelves along the way. Her motorcycle gloves would have protected her hands, but they were back with her bike and her knife. When she left home that morning, she hadn't planned to be trapped in a dark cellar, sitting on roach bodies and groping along a dirty shelf while being held prisoner by psycho computer nerds. Next time the situation arose, she'd be more prepared.

"There's an old lamp just to your left," Charley said. "It looks like it might have a little kerosene left."

"Great. Now all we have to do is find a match to light it."

"Light what?" Dawson asked.

"Just thinking out loud. We could sure use a light right now."

"Yeah," Dawson agreed. "A light, a knife, an assault rifle."

"You've got me," Charley said.

Oh, yay.

"I'm free!" Dawson exclaimed. "Thank you, Grant. Now we need to figure out how to get out of this place."

"We'll dig out," Charley said.

Again with the *we.* Digging out was easy enough to say when he could just fly out.

"Let's try the door," Dawson said. "Take my hand, Grant."

"And mine." Amanda fumbled in the general direction of Dawson's voice and finally connected with a small hand. Grant wrapped his fingers around hers in a trusting manner that made her more than ever determined to somehow get them out of there…alive. "Head for those streaks of light."

The three of them stumbled across the floor and up the first couple of steps. Dawson and Amanda lifted their hands to the door. Grant climbed up another step and did the same.

"On three." She counted, and they pushed at the same time. The wood was rough and Amanda felt splinters digging into her palms, but she bunched her shoulder muscles and pushed harder. Later—assuming there was a *later*—she'd deal with a few splinters.

"It's not moving," Dawson finally said. "Maybe if we had a lever."

Or a stick of dynamite. "Let's try one more thing. Go up a couple of steps, turn around, stoop over and put your back against the door."

They pushed with their backs. Grant grunted with the effort. The door seemed to lift a fraction of an inch, or maybe the bones in Amanda's back lowered a fraction of an inch. The latter seemed more likely.

"I told you they put heavy stuff on it," Charley said. "Forget the door. You can dig out. That crazy woman shot a hole in the wall, and it looks like the concrete grout around the rocks is loose anyway."

Amanda sighed. "This isn't working. We need to try something else."

"The grout between those rocks is pretty old," Grant said. "It's probably loose and crumbly. The stones are big enough, if we could get a couple of them out, I could crawl through and open the door. Surely we can find something in here to dig with."

That was a little freaky. If animals could see Charley, maybe kids could hear him on some level.

Amanda didn't really believe they could dig out of the place, certainly not before Scott and his buddies came back for them, but they might as well be doing something while they waited, anything to divert them from thoughts of dying at the hands of those evil people. "It's worth a shot," she agreed.

Charley smiled. "Told you so."

"I came in here with a piece of broken pipe. That might be a good tool."

"The glass from your phone, gorilla glass, we could use that too," Grant said. "It's very strong."

"Now all we have to do is feel around on this floor until we find all those things." Amanda started to the spot where she thought she'd dropped the pipe.

Charley moved to her side and pointed downward. "It's right there."

She reached to the floor, groped and found it. "I've got the pipe."

"Great!" Dawson said. "You really have a good sense of direction."

"Or a good guide," Charley said.

"Now we need to find the glass and the bullet hole in the wall."

"My pleasure." He crossed to where she'd thrown her phone and looked down. "It's in two pieces. That was some throw, Amanda. I'm sure glad you never decided to punch me. Okay, I'm going to put my hands on the pieces and you can just saunter over, reach down casually and pick them up."

Amanda stumbled through the darkness to where he squatted. She reached through his fingers and found the first piece of glass then the second. "Got it."

"That's incredible, Amanda," Dawson said. "It's almost like you can see in the dark."

Charley was going to be impossible to live with after this.

Dawson and Grant approached, and she gave each of them a piece of the jagged glass. "Now we just need to find that place in the rock where the bullet hit."

"I saw where it went," Grant said. "I can find it." He pushed past Amanda to reach the wall.

"I'll search too," Amanda said, giving Charley a meaningful look.

He smiled, turned to the wall and laid his hand on a certain spot.

"Oh, that's cold!" Grant said, and Amanda figured he'd found Charley's hand.

"That's probably the place," she said. "Bullet exposed the layers of rock inside, and they're colder."

"Really? I never heard that about the inside of a rock being noticeably colder," Dawson said.

"It must be true," Grant said. "I think this is the place. There's a hole in the rock, and the concrete is loose."

"Okay, you dig out the grout on that side," Amanda instructed. "I'll work on the other side and Dawson can take the top."

Charley moved through her and laid his arm along a straight line. "Dig here, Amanda. Go ahead. Don't worry about hurting me. Just dig through my arm. For you, I can take the pain."

"Can the melodrama," she whispered then whacked the rock as hard as she could.

'Ow, ow, ow!" Charley laughed. "Just kidding."

Amanda began to dig at the grout between the stones. It came away with surprising ease.

"My side's really crumbly," Grant said. "It's coming out in big chunks."

"Here too," Dawson replied.

For what seemed like hours but was, Charley assured her, only a few minutes, the three of them worked at the grout around their targeted rock.

"You should be able to pry it out now," Charley said. "The space around the bullet hole is plenty big to get your piece of pipe in for leverage."

"I think we're ready to take out the rock," Amanda said. "I'll just stick this piece of pipe in the hole from the gunshot and we'll lever it out."

Guided by Charley, she found the hole on her first try.

"You're going to owe me big time after this," he said.

That comment actually made Amanda feel better. A Charley who helped her selflessly wasn't the Charley she knew.

With the three of them pushing on the end of the pipe, the rock slowly began to move.

"Keep going," Charley encouraged. "It's stuck to the dirt behind, but it's coming loose."

"There's dirt on the other side?" Of course there was. She remembered the weed-covered mound.

"Yes," Dawson said. "They cover cellars with dirt. A smooth, rounded structure allows the tornado winds to flow over without causing damage."

Suddenly the rock came free of the wall and crashed to the floor.

"Yay!" Amanda groped for Dawson and Grant, hugging them both. Charley tried to join in the group hug but only succeeded in making them shiver and pull apart. Amanda astonished herself by feeling a little sorry for him.

He stepped back. "Now the dirt. It's only about four inches thick right there."

They took turns hacking at the substance that was harder than the concrete they'd just dug out. Four inches of solidly packed Texas earth entangled with the roots of weeds tough enough to survive in the rugged terrain.

"I see daylight!" Dawson exclaimed.

The hole was small, but after being in the dark so long, the glow was almost painful though completely wonderful.

"Keep digging!" she shouted exultantly. "All we have to do is get one more rock loose! The second should be easier!" Freedom was in sight. This might actually work.

The hole widened rapidly and the interior of the cellar became light enough to see each other. Amanda gave a punch with the pipe and took out another clod of dirt. She turned to look at Dawson and Grant and laughed from the sheer joy of the simple experience of sight. "You're beautiful," she said. "Both of you!"

"Both? What about me?" Charley sounded hurt, but he was good at doing that when the occasion called for it. Nevertheless, he had helped.

"You're all beautiful!"

She leaned closer to the hole and drew in a deep breath, expelling the musty, rotting smells of the cellar from her lungs, drinking in the clean scents of dust and sunshine and open spaces.

"Destroying property? I believe that's a criminal offense." Scott leaned over and peered inside.

Chapter Nineteen

Amanda's heart sank to the very ends of her toenails. She'd gone from thinking the plan of digging out had no chance, was something to keep them occupied so they wouldn't think about what was going to happen, to believing freedom was within their reach. Then Scott's grinning face had robbed them of any possibility of freedom.

A dark anger swelled inside her. The man had no right to be there, no right to keep them prisoner and certainly no right to terrify them by threatening their lives.

She lifted her rusty piece of pipe, took aim and stabbed through the hole as hard as she could. The pipe connected with a satisfying thud that shuddered up her arm. Scott fell backward, howled in pain and cursed.

Amanda felt a brief rush of exultation before the Glock appeared in the opening. Damn! She whacked the gun sideways with her pipe just as Alice squeezed the trigger. The bullet went somewhere outside, off to the left.

"Get down!" she shouted, shoving Dawson and Grant to one side of the opening and flattening herself against the other side. The crazy woman could start shooting wildly at any minute.

Charley huddled next to her against the wall. She looked at him, and he grinned sheepishly. "Habit."

She wondered how many bullets he'd dodged in his lifetime that it had become a habit.

"Roger's going to open the door," Scott called, "and you three are going to walk out like compliant captives. If you bring whatever you hit me with, Alice will shoot you. If you do anything stupid, Alice will shoot you. If you anger me, Alice will shoot you. Alice has become quite fond of that gun and would really like to shoot you anyway, so I suggest you walk out with empty hands at your sides and pleasant expressions on your faces."

Scott's calm words chilled Amanda more than passing through Charley would have. If Roger was back and Scott was calm, that probably meant he hadn't spotted Jake and Ross coming down the road, rushing to the rescue. Not good.

But she wasn't going to give up without a fight. She considered hiding the piece of pipe on her person, but that was the downside of wearing tight jeans. No room to hide weapons.

From outside metal scraped and clunked across the wooden door. Abruptly it lifted, allowing the evening sunlight to flood the room.

Dawson and Grant blinked in the sudden glare and looked at Amanda as if expecting her to tell them what to do. Great. When had they held a meeting and elected her the leader? Of all the things she was not qualified for, taking charge of a life and death situation ranked right up there with singing for the Metropolitan Opera.

"We're coming out quietly," she said. "I'm putting down my weapon." She laid the piece of pipe on the floor then walked as steadily as possible toward the light of the open door, pretending to be brave and hoping to give Dawson and Grant courage by her phony example.

If Scott was using the threat of Alice shooting them to make them come out rather than just killing them in the cellar, that must mean they believed her story that Dawson knew the location of the program they wanted so badly. Of course, since he didn't know, they were only buying time.

She straightened her spine and met Roger's gaze unflinchingly as she moved up the steps. So they were buying time. Every minute they delayed gave them a chance to figure a way out. This wasn't over until the crazy woman actually hit somebody with that Glock.

"Check her to be sure she doesn't have any more sharp objects," Scott said.

Amanda turned to look at him and smiled. She'd given him an ugly, bloody wound in his cheek. "You might want to check into getting a tetanus shot. That pipe was really rusty."

Scott's eyes narrowed to slits and Amanda thought—hoped—she could see the blood pulsing angrily and painfully behind his injury.

"You really need to keep your mouth shut and back off," he said. "Your friend has something I need. You don't. You're expendable."

"And you're—"

213

"Amanda!" Charley interrupted. "For once in your life, think before you open your mouth!"

Dawson moved up beside her. "Do what he says."

At first she thought he was telling her to take Charley's advice but then realized he was referring to Scott's orders. She lifted her arms and held her hands out to show Roger she had no weapons.

He made a tentative move toward her as if he was thinking about doing a pat-down. Charley punched him in the face.

Roger looked startled, lifted his hand to his nose and backed up. "She doesn't have anything," he assured Scott.

Scott nodded toward the back porch. "Inside."

Making a determined effort to stomp along in her boots rather than shake in them, Amanda led the way up the rickety wooden steps, through a door that dangled from one hinge and into what had once been a kitchen. It still held a stained sink under a broken window, another ladder back chair with only three legs and a drop leaf table missing one leaf. Straw, dirt and bird droppings littered the floor, but light streamed in through the dirty, broken windows. For that reason, it was a better place to be than the cellar.

"Keep going," Scott ordered. "We've got the laptops set up in the living room."

That room was slightly cleaner than the kitchen. A dilapidated sofa and chair had been shoved against one wall and the middle of the floor had been swept. Three sleeping bags were rolled and waiting along the wall. Four laptops were set up on a clean folding table with three folding chairs.

Dawson would be expected to produce the program, and then they'd all be killed as his parents had been. Actually, they'd probably die slow, horrible deaths with Alice taking several shots to kill each of them. Amanda wondered if the woman had enough bullets to finish the job considering how bad her aim was. Maybe they'd just bleed to death in excruciating pain.

As unofficial leader, she had to come up with some way to keep that from happening, but at the moment she was fresh out of ideas.

Scott waved a hand toward the table where the laptops sat surrounded by soda cans and fast food wrappers with a brown purse on the far end. "Come up with that code or you belong to Alice."

Dawson and Grant sank down on two of the chairs and looked at each other then at Amanda. She didn't see much in the way of weapons. An empty aluminum can didn't have the same potential as a broken beer bottle. The purse which probably belonged to Alice might contain something she could use, but the woman would shoot her before she had a chance to empty its contents and look.

"Now would be a good time to come up with a new plan," Charley said. "Don't think of them as crazed murderers. Think of them as your dad when you get in trouble and he's about to punish you."

Amanda had usually been able to wrap her stern father around her little finger, but her mother had been a whole other story. Her best defense against that woman had always been a good offense.

"Go ahead, Dawson. Give them the code. I know you don't want to, but we don't have a choice." With no enthusiasm Dawson pulled one of the laptops over to him and cast Amanda a terrified glance. She turned her attention back to Scott and gathered her courage, determined to be offensive. "I am sick to death of hearing about this stinking code. What does this program do that's so freaking important you've killed people and ruined lives to get it? What the heck is Project Verdant? Pardon me if I don't buy into this business of your being skilled programmers. If you're so great, why don't you just write your own program? What's so special about this one?"

"Doesn't your friend here know all about it? Didn't his father leave him a letter?" Scott asked. "Or was that another lie?"

Oops. "He knows where the code is. That's all that was in the letter. He doesn't know what it does. You have put us all through hell and you're going to kill us because of this stupid program. The least you can do is tell us what is so freaking special about it."

"Fine." Scott pulled out the third chair and sat down, laying the gun on the table. Alice grabbed it immediately. She really did have a thing for that Glock.

Grant rose. "Sit here, Amanda."

"Thank you, Grant. That's very sweet of you, but I'm okay." She preferred to be on her feet, ready to run.

The boy stood rigidly beside the chair. "I'd feel better if you'd sit."

Such polite manners. Or maybe he just didn't want to be at the table with Scott. She couldn't blame him for that. She walked over to the chair, telling herself to keep her cool and pretend they were at a dinner party, not a murder party. Grant reached for her hand and she took his, intending to clasp it in a reassuring grip, but she felt something sharp in his palm. She flinched and almost drew back but then realized he was trying to hand her his piece of broken gorilla glass from her cell phone.

She folded her fingers around the glass and accepted it along with the responsibility it implied. He was counting on her to save them.

She sank down on the chair and leaned toward Scott in an attempt to distract his attention from Dawson's flustered and unproductive efforts on the computer.

"So why can't you write your own program if you're such hotshot techno-nerds?"

She sensed Alice move up behind her an instant before the side of her face exploded in pain.

"You bitch!" Charley shouted, his hand sweeping futilely through Alice's hand that held the Glock. "Are you all right, Amanda?"

"Alice," Scott said quietly, "that's a gun, not a black jack. Don't get it bloody."

Amanda lifted a hand to her cheek. The skin felt raw, and she wondered if her jaw was broken. She'd been slapped and pistol-whipped by these creeps, and she was starting to get really pissed off. Somehow she'd get out of this alive and she'd teach these assholes some manners.

"We are *hotshot techno-nerds*. We're certified in all the latest programming languages." Alice clutched the gun in both hands. Her voice was bitter. "We were the best at what we did but then some executive with a room temperature IQ decided to outsource our jobs to India so he and his buddies could get two million dollar bonuses every year instead of just one million."

Silence filled the room. This was obviously important, but Amanda couldn't see how it related to the current situation. "Okay, that sucks. But what does that have to do with..." She spread her hands in a gesture encompassing the room, the computers, all of them.

"We didn't take it lying down," Alice said. "We didn't go on unemployment, and we didn't settle for jobs we were over-qualified for. We took what we were entitled to." She shot an angry look at Dawson. "Until your father interfered and ruined everything."

Dawson looked up at her, his fingers on the keyboard motionless. "My dad never hurt anybody."

"Yes," Roger said. "He did. He cut off our source of income."

Dawson shook his head. "He was a college professor. He didn't fire people or outsource jobs to India."

Alice snorted. "He might as well have. Project Verdant. Green. Money. We were taking what we deserved directly from the people who owed it to us, the country that should have protected our jobs and didn't."

Amanda glanced at Dawson. He looked as confused as she felt. "You stole from the government?" she asked. "What does that mean? You didn't pay your taxes? You filed a phony FEMA claim?"

Alice made a noise that sounded as if she'd just laid an egg. Amanda finally decided it was supposed to be a laugh. "We used our skills. We wrote a program to take the salaries we should be earning directly from the Federal Reserve System." She and Roger both beamed with pride at their accomplishment. Even Scott started to smile but then changed to a frown when the movement reached the raw wound on his cheek. He wouldn't be able to smirk for a while without pain.

"You hacked into the Federal Reserve System?" Dawson sounded astonished and, she thought, a little impressed.

"We were entitled to that money," Roger said. "Your father had no right to stop us from getting it. His actions were just as bad as sending our jobs overseas."

Dawson shook his head. "I don't understand. My dad taught economics. What did he have to do with the Federal Reserve System?"

"Your mother," Scott said. "She noticed something at the bank where she worked and told him to check it out. He found our program and tried to report us. Fortunately, we were tracking him from the minute he touched our code, so we intercepted that call. I posed as a treasury agent and met with him."

Dawson looked thoughtful. "That's what he meant about contacting the authorities but not trusting them."

Scott's lips thinned and his eyes narrowed. "He wouldn't leave it alone. I told him we'd take care of it, but he got impatient and went behind my back to write a program to block ours and stop the transfer of money."

The insanity was starting to make sense. Dawson and Grant's father had stopped them from stealing from the Federal Reserve. Cut off their income as surely as their former employers when they sent their jobs to India. This entire nightmare came down to money and ego. Dawson and Grant lost their parents because these arrogant jerks thought it was beneath them to take a cut in pay, to look for a job like regular people.

"So write another program and steal from somebody else, a bank or something."

Alice stepped closer and Amanda flinched, fearful the woman was going to hit her again. "What do you think we are? Common thieves? We'd never steal from a bank. We only want what we're entitled to."

"Okay, you're not common thieves, but you're murderers and not very bright ones. You killed Dawson's parents. If you were all that smart, you'd have made his father take down the program first. You're not smart. You're dumb and evil."

"Amanda!" Charley protested. "It's not a good idea to insult somebody who has a gun."

Alice lifted the Glock again. "We're all members of Mensa, something you could certainly never hope to achieve."

Amanda raised her chin defiantly. "I'm a member of the NRA."

Alice snickered. "That doesn't help you much when I've got the gun, does it?"

"Maybe you've got the gun, but we've got the program." She met Alice's gaze defiantly. "You kill us the way you killed Dawson's parents and you still won't have that program. And Mensa will revoke your membership because that would be a really dumb thing to do."

"How's Mensa going to find out they did that if you're dead?" Charley asked.

Amanda ignored him.

Scott let out a long sigh. "We thought we had the code when we killed the Dawsons. I told Professor Dawson the FBI's IT department was about to break the code that transferred money but his program was interfering with our progress. He gave me a flash drive that he said contained the source code. By the time we figured out he'd given us bogus code, we'd already blown up him and his wife. We thought those two kids would be in the car too. But I guess it's a good thing they weren't since their father lied to us."

"I see. You thought you had the program and you killed Dawson's parents. Why should Dawson give you the program if you're going to kill us when he does?"

Scott nodded. "That's a valid question. We'll make you a deal. You give us the program, we verify it's the right one, then we take both vehicles, leaving you stranded but alive. By the time you get back to civilization, we'll be in Belize with our income restored, living under false identities."

"Don't believe him, Amanda!" Charley darted between Scott and Amanda. "He's got that tone in his voice and that look in his eyes. Do not trust him."

"I know," Amanda replied quietly. But it was a way to buy more time. Every minute was another chance.

"You know what?" Scott asked.

"I know a good deal when I hear one." She tried to smile, but the corners of her mouth refused to go up. She was probably grimacing like some sort of ghoul. "You put that in writing, Dawson will give you the program, and we'll all live happily ever after." Assuming you defined *ever after* as five minutes. She looked at Charley and spread her hands in a *help me* gesture.

"Create a diversion and run for it," Charley advised.

Great advice. She'd just toss a bomb in the corner and run away as fast as she could in her motorcycle boots. Oh, wait, she didn't have a bomb. She glared at Charley, wishing she dared tell him how ridiculous his suggestion was.

"You want it in writing?" Scott scowled, lifted his hands in confusion and looked around the room. "That's insane. You're not getting it in writing."

Amanda folded her arms. Kept them from shaking. "If you're being honest about that deal, you won't have a problem putting it in writing."

Scott studied her for a long moment as if trying to decide whether she was really that crazy. By that point she probably looked crazy. She certainly felt it. "Look around you. We don't have a printer," he finally said.

"Who needs a printer in the digital age? You've got four computers." She grabbed the nearest one, spun it over to her and hit the touch pad to bring it out of sleep mode. It was Grant's computer with all the games and the defective audio program. That might provide a small diversion. It wasn't a bomb, but it was all she had.

She clicked on the icon for the music program then shot up from her chair when the same hideous noise as before burst into the room. She lunged toward Scott, aiming for his already-wounded cheek, gouging with the glass. He screamed and grabbed his face.

She whirled around in time to see Dawson throw himself on Roger, taking both of them to the floor.

"Grab the purse!" Charley shouted in her ear, trying to make himself heard over the noise coming from the laptop. "It's got a set of car keys in it!"

Roger screamed, clutching his neck as red oozed between his fingers. Dawson had apparently saved his piece of gorilla glass too.

From the corner of her eye Amanda saw Alice raise the Glock.

"I got this one!" Charley darted through Alice. She gasped and shivered, momentarily lowering the gun.

Amanda grabbed the brown purse from the table with one hand and with the other slashed at Alice's arm with the glass. "Run!" she shouted, hoping Dawson and Grant could hear her over the racket.

"Over here!" Grant yanked the front door open.

Amanda tossed the bag toward him. "Car keys!" He caught the bag like the baseball player he was and fumbled inside as he ran out onto the porch.

Dawson disentangled himself from Roger, dodged past Alice and lunged for Grant's laptop, slamming it shut and stopping the noise. He dropped his piece of glass, snatched up the computer and headed for the door.

Scott seized Amanda's arm. She spun on him and drew the gorilla glass down the other side of his face. He cursed but didn't release his grip.

Dawson turned back.

"No, go!" she shouted.

Of course he didn't go. Nobody ever listened to her.

He dropped the computer and threw himself at Scott. It wasn't exactly a football tackle, but Scott didn't seem to be in any better shape than Dawson. The battle of the nerds.

"Hold it!" Alice shouted.

That damn gun again. Amanda had had about enough of that.

Unlike Dawson and Scott, she had played a little neighborhood football in her childhood. She dove for

Alice's legs at the same time Charley darted through the woman. Alice thudded to the floor.

"Get the gun!" Charley shouted. "Three feet to your right!"

Amanda rolled, spotted the Glock and grabbed it. She fired a shot through the ceiling as she scrambled to her feet. She had everyone's attention.

Dawson and Scott broke apart. Scott rose to his feet and started toward her. Amanda took a step backward but leveled the gun at him. "I'm not Alice. I know how to use this. NRA, not Mensa, remember?"

Dawson grabbed the laptop off the floor.

"Forget the damn computer! Get out of here!"

Scott lunged and Amanda hesitated only a split second before she fired a shot into his shoulder. Probably should have aimed for the crotch. He yelped and fell forward, knocking the gun out of her hand.

"Alice is on her feet!" Charley warned at the same time Amanda felt a hand grasp her shoulder.

She shrugged off the hand and turned to look for the gun.

"Get out now!" Charley shouted.

Once in a while Charley was right. Amanda ran from the house.

Grant already sat in the back seat of the sedan. Dawson was climbing into the passenger side, and the driver's door was open with the engine running. Amanda slid inside, threw the car into gear and screeched out of the yard onto the dusty, rutted road.

Charley dropped on the console between the seats. "Faster, Amanda! They're coming after you in the van!"

Amanda glanced in the rearview mirror but couldn't see anything for the dust.

A bullet shattered the side mirror.

Chapter Twenty

Amanda floored the gas pedal and held on tightly to the steering wheel as the car bounced over the rutted road leaving a cloud of dust behind. The rough road would probably ruin the entire suspension system as well as the front end ball joints. Maybe blow out a tire or two. Not that she cared if this car got totally destroyed and the psychotic trio's insurance had lapsed the day before. That would serve them right. She just hoped it didn't break down before she and the boys made their getaway in it. As long as the car held together, surely she could out-drive a minivan.

She twisted the wheel and spun around a curve, hanging on with both hands as she was thrown into Charley.

"I don't mind if you want to cuddle," Charley said, "but this probably isn't the right time."

"Everybody okay?" she asked.

"I'm fine," Grant said from the back seat.

"Yes." From the corner of her eye she could see Dawson clutching the laptop with one hand and the dashboard with the other.

Another explosion sounded and the car spun out of control. Had Alice shot a tire while aiming for the back window or had something else gone wrong with the car? It didn't matter. All that mattered was bringing the car to a safe stop and then—she had no idea what then. One emergency at a time.

She pumped the brake and focused all her strength, mental and physical, on getting control as the car lurched off the road and over the rocky ground. Finally it came to a stop next to a gnarled mesquite tree several feet from the road. The damned minivan pulled in behind them like an unpaid speeding ticket that just wouldn't go away. Panic clenched her insides and paralyzed her limbs. She pushed it back. Later she'd freak out, indulge her fears and slam several Cokes in a row. Right now Dawson and Grant were depending on her. She was depending on her.

"Check the glove box. See if there's something we can use for a weapon in there. I'll check the trunk." Amanda hit the button to release the trunk then opened her door and stepped out. A car jack wouldn't be as good as a gun, but it was better than nothing. "Stay in there, Grant!" she yelled when the boy's door started to open.

He ignored her and scrambled out.

"Nothing in the glove box but a half-eaten package of Cheetos." Dawson got out, slammed his door and headed for the rear of the car.

Amanda stumbled through the clumps of grass and weeds to the trunk then threw up the lid.

Empty.

"It'll be under the carpet," Grant said. "Pull up the edge."

She and Dawson each reached for one side of the carpet lining just as a bullet slammed into the side of the car.

"Get over here, all of you," Scott shouted.

Charley appeared beside her. "I think you're in trouble."

She slammed the lid. "What happened to *we*? All of a sudden it's just me?"

"No," Dawson said, giving her a curious look. "He said all of us."

"Yeah, well, I'm already dead." It was the first time Charley sounded happy about being dead.

Scott, Roger and Alice stood in front of the van. They were, Amanda was pleased to notice, bloody and bruised, but they did not look beaten.

Anger and fear shared equal knots in Amanda's gut. It was hard to keep a positive attitude when she was running out of options. She picked up a rock. Like Sundance and Butch, she'd go down fighting, even if her only weapon was a rock.

"Get that laptop out of the car," Scott ordered. "As much trouble as you went to saving it, that's got to be the one with the code."

Dawson stepped back, reached in and lifted out the computer.

"Is it?" Amanda asked. "Is it the one?"

He bit his lip and nodded. "That music, it's computer generated, the first music program I ever wrote. It's horrible. Dad would never have put it on Grant's computer like that except to mark the spot."

"And it's impossible to change to another selection," Amanda said. "I tried."

"I never used that to play my music." Grant moved up beside her. "Dad put it on there, but I never used it. I always used iTunes. He knew that."

"Well," Amanda said. "I'm glad we finally found that freaking source code."

"You are?" Charley asked. "Why?"

"Sarcasm," Amanda hissed.

"I'll hit them with the laptop," Dawson whispered as the three of them moved across the few feet of stubbled ground separating them from probable death. One ghost, one child, one woman with a rock, and one nerd with a laptop against three killers and a gun. The odds didn't seem favorable.

The theme from *High Noon* played through Amanda's head as she walked on wooden legs toward the van.

We're going to die. The thought rolled through her mind with a frigid intensity, stirring her anger. She could at least see to it the evil trio didn't get what they wanted.

She looked at Charley. "Can you erase it?"

"Sure," Dawson replied, assuming she was speaking to him. "I could erase the whole hard drive if I had a couple of minutes. Do you have a plan?"

Charley shrugged. "I don't know."

"Try! Dawson, hold the laptop out in front of you. This may hurt."

"What?"

She snatched the computer from him and tossed it to the ground. "Do it!"

Charley squatted and reached inside with both hands.

"Get it!" Scott shouted.

Roger ran over and reached down for the computer. Charley threw himself on top of it. Sparks sizzled from the laptop. Roger screamed and jumped back.

"You may kill us, but you're not going to get your damned program!" she shouted. "It's gone! Erased! Fried! Suck it up and apply for a real job at Burger King!" Wielding her rock, she charged toward them. Before she died, she'd do her best to cause these people as much pain as possible. "Remember the Alamo!"

Alice lifted the gun, her finger on the trigger.

A rumbling, rattling sound came from behind Amanda. She spun around to see a car followed by a cloud of dust barreling down the road. The vehicle was covered in dirt and rattled ominously as if it would fall apart at any minute, but it was the most beautiful car Amanda had ever seen.

She changed direction and headed for the road. "Help! Help!" She threw the rock, hitting the car on the fender. She had to get the driver's attention. Later she'd worry about car repairs and whether her insurance company would cancel her for rocking another vehicle.

The car swerved around and screeched to a stop behind the van. Both front doors flew open and two men stepped out. Jake and Ross! The cavalry had arrived!

"They're getting away!" Charley shouted.

Scott, Roger and Alice were scrambling back into the van. The engine roared to life and the

231

minivan shot onto the road. Jake and Ross turned back toward their car but before they could get in, the sound of metal colliding with metal shrieked through the air. The minivan had collided head-on with another vehicle, a bulky car that was probably white under all the dirt and dust.

The driver's side door of that car opened and a slim woman with bright hair emerged. Sunny! All the cavalry had arrived! Amanda started to laugh but the sound merged with a sob somewhere halfway up her throat.

"Police!" Jake shouted, and she turned her attention to him. Gun drawn, he approached the driver's side of the van.

Ross, also holding a gun, circled around to the passenger side. "Get out with your hands behind your head."

Amanda wanted to run over to Jake and throw her arms around his neck, then to Ross, then Sunny and Dawson and Grant, and then maybe she'd even hug Charley.

Or maybe not.

"The woman in the van has a gun!" she shouted to Jake and Ross. "And she's crazy!"

Time froze. No sound or movement came from the van. The loud chaos of the past few minutes was replaced with a preternatural silence. The dust on the road settled quietly to the ground. Heat waves shimmered through the air with no breeze to disperse them. Tendrils of smoke drifted slowly upward from the laptop where it lay in the dirt. The squawk of a grackle in a nearby locust tree sounded loud enough to be heard in the next county.

As if that squawk somehow broke the spell, the back passenger door of the van slid open and Alice tossed out her gun. It landed in the dirt with a quiet plop.

The front doors opened slowly. With no fanfare the three people who had murdered Dawson's parents and his neighbor then traumatized and terrorized Dawson and Grant stepped outside with their hands locked behind their heads.

Somehow it seemed anti-climactic. Considering everything these people had done, Amanda had expected them to come out with guns blazing, never mind they only had one gun and must be running out of ammo.

"Other side of the vehicle, over there with your buddy," Jake instructed Scott and Alice. "Please do something stupid because I'd really love to have an excuse to shoot you."

Scott looked at the laptop. Wisps of smoke still trailed from it but were becoming fainter. He shook his head and sighed. "We're not going to do anything. It doesn't matter now. It's all over."

"I do not freaking believe you people!" Amanda strode up to him. "The three of you could have done so many things with your abilities but you threw your lives away because you couldn't steal from the government anymore?"

Scott flinched backward. "Get her away from me." He lifted a hand to his shoulder. "She assaulted me and then shot me!"

Jake didn't take his eyes off Scott and Alice, but he grinned. "You know what they say. Don't mess with Texas women."

Amanda's would like to assault Scott again, but that probably wouldn't be a good idea with two cops around. "There's a vacant house a couple of miles farther down the road. That's where they held us captive and tortured us."

"Tortured you? Oh, look at your poor face!"

Amanda spun around at the sound of that voice. "Mother?" She'd have sworn nothing could surprise her after everything that had happened, but the sight of prim and proper Beverly Caulfield wearing tan slacks and a silk blouse, every hair in place, her designer heels covered in dust, was not something she'd have expected in her wildest dreams.

Beverly frowned. "Are these the people who hurt you?"

Amanda had forgotten her own injuries in the adrenalin of the situation. "Yes. Mother, what are you doing here?"

"We came in her car." Sunny moved up to her other side, hand held close to her dark skirt, almost hiding a Colt Mustang .380. "She's the reason we're all here."

Amanda looked at Sunny then at her mother, two women who couldn't be more different yet each qualified as *mother* in her life. "Mom let you drive her Mercedes? Did you threaten to tell the world she uses paper napkins?"

"Don't be absurd. I would never use paper napkins. I asked Sunny to drive because she drives faster than I do."

"Yeah, most people do." Including ninety year old men on their way home from a heart transplant.

"Detective Daggett," Beverly Caulfield said, "we wish to press charges against this man for assaulting my daughter."

Jake blinked rapidly but maintained his composure. "We'll look into that."

"Yes, you will. He will pay for hurting my daughter." She lifted a hand to Amanda's face, close enough Amanda could feel her warmth but not quite touching.

"I'm okay." Amanda tried to push her mother's fingers aside, but Beverly grabbed her wrist and turned it palms-up.

"What happened to your hand?"

"It's just a few splinters. I'm okay, really."

"We'll get Wendell Langston to take care of you."

"Mom! Doctor Langston's a brain surgeon. He's not going to treat my scratches."

"Of course he will. He plays golf with your father." She moved over to Dawson and Grant, somehow managing to be graceful even in three-inch heels on uneven, rocky ground.

"Dawson, it's lovely to see you again. I don't believe I've met your brother. You must be Grant. Sunny filled me in on the situation while we drove here. I'm Beverly Caulfield, Amanda's mother." She extended a manicured hand.

Grant wiped his hand on his jeans then accepted Beverly's in a tentative shake. "Hi. Uh, nice to meet you."

"Are either of you hurt?"

"No." Dawson moved his bruised wrists behind his back, and Grant shook his head vehemently. Apparently neither of them wanted to be treated by a neurosurgeon.

Jake gave Amanda a helpless look then grasped Scott's shoulder and spun him around. "Over there."

Scott and Alice trudged to the other side of the van to join Roger. While Jake kept his gun trained on them, Ross slapped handcuffs on the three and shoved them into the backseat of the car with the dented fender.

Jake came over to Amanda. "I'll need you all to come down to the station and give statements."

Beverly stepped between Jake and her. "She needs to see a doctor first."

Amanda leaned around her mother. "No, she doesn't."

"Tomorrow will be fine." He looked at Dawson and Grant then back to her. "I think all of you could use a good night's rest."

He was right. Dawson had aged ten years and had dark circles under his eyes. Grant was haggard and worn in a way no eleven year old boy should ever be. They stood together, separate from everyone else, alone, back in their small world.

That wasn't going to happen.

Amanda strode over, pushed between them and wrapped an arm around each boy. "We'll all look, feel, and smell better after a shower, some food and a good night's sleep. And I know a house with extra bathrooms and bedrooms as well as maid service. We can even ride there in a Mercedes." Amanda looked directly at her mother, daring her to refuse. She'd see just how far she could push the woman's southern hospitality.

Beverly didn't blink. "I'll call Lucinda and have her set three extra places." She turned toward Sunny. "Four if you will join us."

Amanda had to give her mother bonus points. Opening her home to two strangers was commendable, but including her daughter's birth mother, her husband's former lover, was going the extra mile.

Sunny's eyes widened and she took a step backward. "Uh—"

"Of course she will." Two friends, one father and two mothers. That sounded like a good mix to Amanda. An evening with those people and a couple of Cokes should help her heal from the awful memories of the past few hours.

"We'll stop by Dawson's apartment and get clean clothes for you boys," Beverly said, moving onward with her plans as if the possibility of a refusal was simply not possible.

Amanda tried to recall if she'd ever known anyone to refuse her mother. Not in her lifetime.

"Okay," Jake said, "that's settled. Tomorrow morning I'll see Amanda, Dawson, and Grant at the station."

"Tomorrow afternoon," Amanda corrected. "My bike's around here somewhere, out of gas. I need to get my purse tonight, but I don't think I'm up to riding right now so I'll come back for it tomorrow."

"Come by the station early, we'll get the statement out of the way and I'll bring you out here with a gas can." Jake spoke the words casually as if tossing out an offhand solution to a problem.

It didn't sound offhand and casual to Amanda. It sounded like another opportunity for the two of them to sit in his car. Maybe this time she could figure out a way to make Charley stay outside. "That'll work." Her reply was just as casual and offhand and full of import as his.

"Good. Right now I'm going to take these people in and let Ross and his team come back and process that house and these two vehicles."

"Oh, that reminds me. There may be a body in that van."

Beverly gasped. Sunny flinched. Jake scowled. "A body? As in a dead person?"

"Well, at least they said there is. I can't swear to it. I haven't seen it with my own eyes. But they said it's the real Brendan Matthews."

"The real Brendan Matthews? So he's been dead at least two days."

"Three."

Jake looked toward the horizon where the hot summer sun was starting to set. "Ross isn't going to enjoy collecting this evidence. He's probably going to have to take a couple of showers and use cologne before his date tonight with Hannah."

"At least now he knows for sure that Hannah's innocent."

Jake laughed. "Yeah, he was pretty worried about that."

"I think that's sarcasm again," Charley said.

"Get over here or I'm leaving without you," Ross called.

"On my way!" Jake's dark gaze settled on Amanda and he moved a fraction of an inch closer. "You really should get those cuts checked out."

"We'll see."

He lifted a hand and for a brief moment she thought he was going to touch her.

Of course he wasn't. Not in front of a bazillion people.

But if no one else had been there...

"Okay." He stepped back. "Tomorrow. At the station." He turned and headed to the police car where Ross waited and the perps sweated.

She'd probably imagined that he almost touched her. Wishful thinking. A trick of the fading light of evening.

"I thought he was going to touch your face," Charley said. "You need to be careful of him. I don't think you should ride out here alone with him tomorrow."

So she hadn't imagined it. She smiled and watched Jake walking toward the car. In spite of the odds, he'd managed to find her and rush in to save her life. And that brought up a question.

"How did you know?" she called after him. "How did you know where to find us?"

"Ask your mother." He got in the car, started the engine and pulled around the sturdy Mercedes with its scratched paint and the van with a crumpled front end.

Ask your mother?

Which one?

She looked around to see Beverly beside her car, studying the point of impact. "With all this dust, it's hard to tell how much damage those people did. And driving so fast over this awful road probably ruined my car. I didn't even know they had roads like this in Texas. I'm going to speak with someone about it."

Sunny and Amanda looked at each other and rolled their eyes.

"It'll be fine, Beverly," Sunny said. "Your car is much sturdier than that minivan, and you have good insurance."

"Let's get in and start the air conditioning," Amanda suggested, reaching for the rear door handle. "In you go, Dawson. You get to sit in the middle, Grant, because you're a kid and kids have no choices."

Dawson started toward the open door then stopped and looked back at the laptop. "How did you do that?"

"Do what?"

"The sparks," Grant said, peering at the black rectangle which now lay quietly in the dust, no longer emitting smoke or any sign of life. "You weren't even close to it when it blew up."

Charley took a bow.

"Bad battery," Amanda said. "Exploded when I threw it on the ground."

"But you warned me to hold it away from me, that it might hurt," Dawson protested. "That was before it even sparked. How did you know?"

Charley floated over to stand beside the object under discussion. "Go ahead, Amanda. Tell them how you did it. Don't worry about me. I don't need public adulation. Just your private adoration will be fine."

That was so like Charley. Put her in a difficult situation and then gloat about it. She'd tell the world about him if not for the fact the world would think she was nuts the way Sunny had yesterday.

Dawson and Grant waited quietly for an answer. Her mother dusted the Mercedes emblem on her hood with a tissue. Sunny watched Amanda intently as if she too was waiting for an explanation of the inexplicable.

Okay, it wouldn't be a good idea to go with *Charley's ghost* for her explanation. "Adrenalin. We can do amazing things when we're in a critical situation."

Sunny's expression said she knew Amanda was lying.

Beverly completed her dusting and moved to the driver's side door. "I'll drive this time. We're in no hurry and while I am very grateful that you were able to drive fast enough to save my—our daughter, I believe my car and I will both feel more comfortable with me at the wheel."

Sunny nodded slowly and went to the passenger side.

Amanda, Dawson and Grant slid into the back seat. For the first time Amanda was glad her mother had such stodgy taste in cars. The heavy Mercedes had survived the crash with only cosmetic damage, was still drivable after the race over *this awful road*, and had enough room in the back seat for the three of them.

"We need to stop just a little way up the road so I can get my purse, helmet and jacket," Amanda said.

The engine purred to life and cool air flowed from the vents. The comforts of life had never felt more comfortable.

"How did you know where to find us?" Amanda asked. "I couldn't get cell phone reception, so I thought my GPS didn't work."

"It didn't," Sunny said, "except for that call you made to your mom."

"The call I made to Mom? When I left her a message about the baby shower?"

"No," Beverly said, "the one when you shouted at Charley, telling him to stop."

"I called you and shouted for Charley to stop?"

"You called me, Jake, and your mother," Sunny said, "but neither Jake nor I was available to answer the call, and you didn't leave a message. Your mother was the only one of us who answered, and Jake was able to get a lock on your location from that call."

Charley settled on the console between the seats, facing Amanda. "Remember when I made your cell phone work?" he asked.